"I think you're reading too much into a little moonlight and a root-beer float, Frank,"

Rebecca told him. "I'm not used to getting terribly serious about a man after knowing him only a few days, even though—"

"Even though what?" he asked, moving closer to her.

"I've never felt as much honesty as I feel with you."

Frank looked at her seriously. "I've been as honest with you as I can be, but . . . well, there are things that are better left buried in the past."

"Are you hiding something from me, Frank?" Rebecca asked with a laugh.

He shook his head. "Not as much hiding something as just not making an issue of it."

"I knew it! Dark-haired men *are* dangerous and secretive—even when they're supposed to be angels."

Dear Reader:

Happy holidays! Our authors join me in wishing you all the best for a joyful, loving holiday season with your family and friends. And while celebrating the new year—and the new decade!—I hope you'll think of Silhouette Books.

1990 promises to be especially happy here. This year marks our tenth anniversary, and we're planning a celebration! To symbolize the timelessness of love, as well as the modern gift of the tenth anniversary, each month in 1990, we're presenting readers with a *Diamond Jubilee* Silhouette Romance title, penned by one of your all-time favorite Silhouette Romance authors.

In January, under the Silhouette Romance line's *Diamond Jubilee* emblem, look for Diana Palmer's next book in her bestselling LONG, TALL TEXANS series—*Ethan*. He's a hero sure to lasso your heart! And just in time for Valentine's Day, Brittany Young has written *The Ambassador's Daughter*. Spend the most romantic month of the year in France, the setting for this magical classic. Victoria Glenn, Annette Broadrick, Peggy Webb, Dixie Browning, Phyllis Halldorson—to name just a few!—have written *Diamond Jubilee* titles especially for you. And Pepper Adams has penned a trilogy about three very rugged heroes—and their lovely heroines!—set on the plains of Oklahoma. Look for the first book this summer.

The *Diamond Jubilee* celebration is Silhouette Romance's way of saying thanks to you, our readers. We've been together for ten years now, and with the support you've given us, you can look forward to many more years of heartwarming, poignant love stories.

I hope you'll enjoy this book and all of the stories to come. Come home to romance—Silhouette Romance—for always!

Sincerely,

Tara Hughes Gavin
Senior Editor

JANE BIERCE

Dearly Beloved

Silhouette Romance

Published by Silhouette Books New York

America's Publisher of Contemporary Romance

This book is dedicated
to the loving memory of
Rev. Canon Gerard "Gerry" Rubino,
for his encouragement to me
and kindness to Lynn,
and with deepest thanks
to my paraliterary,
my son Stephen,
who is my researcher,
proofreader, cheerleader
and supplier of
Hershey's Miniatures.
Watch out, Otherworlds!

SILHOUETTE BOOKS
300 E. 42nd St., New York, N.Y. 10017

ISBN: 0-373-08697-0

First Silhouette Books printing January 1990

Printed in the U.S.A.

Books by Jane Bierce

Silhouette Romance

Finishing Touch #594
Dearly Beloved #697

JANE BIERCE,

a native of Pennsylvania, moved to Florida several years ago. Now with her three children grown, she divides her time between writing romances and making quilts. She actively encourages aspiring writers by visiting high school classes and participating in critique groups. Jane loves to curl up with a romance written by Dixie Browning, Glenda Sands or Beverly Sommers.

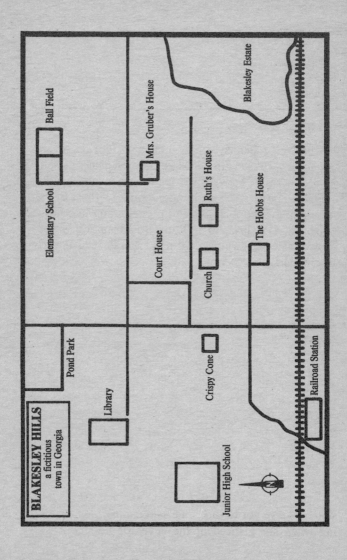

Chapter One

Rebecca Hobbs's heart sank when she walked down the corridor to her office at Halburton Development and saw the firm's vice president, Jonathan Douglas, lounging against the paneled wall beside her locked door. He was tall and blond and handsome, and he was very much at ease in a light gray suit that was obviously from one of the best clothiers in Atlanta and was definitely not off the rack.

Unfortunately, the second thing she'd noticed was the long white envelope in his hand, and she suspected it contained her termination notice. She thought she'd accomplished a major feat when she managed to say a cordial greeting to him and unlock the door at the same time. After all, she had to uphold her reputation for being cool under fire, no matter what it cost her.

Jonathan followed her into her office, his manner casual. "We've got to talk," he said calmly, not even blinking when she glanced at the envelope he still held. She dawdled as she dropped her briefcase on her desk and put her purse in the bottom drawer of her filing cabinet.

"I don't think there's much to talk about," she said, straightening her slender shoulders defensively and taking the envelope from his hand.

"I want to apologize," he said unexpectedly, his tone contrite.

Rebecca looked up at him with surprise in her expressive hazel eyes. "I don't think that's necessary."

"It *is* necessary," Jonathan insisted. "I tried to save your job for you, but George was adamant about retaining the lawyer who's been with Jacobs Properties. He's got twelve years' experience to your two."

His shrug and sigh were sympathetic, Rebecca supposed, but the truth was that he probably had to look out for his own job and couldn't be too protective of her without risking his own future.

She, however, was expendable.

She'd been so proud of her work in putting the merger together, because Claiborne Ballenger, the lawyer for Jacobs Properties, had proved to be a tough negotiator. And all the while Ballenger had made comments that had made it clear he assumed he would be the one lawyer retained as staff counsel!

When George Halburton had begun to respond positively to the other man's comments, Rebecca had suddenly seen how tenuous her position was. She was too numb to be angry, too fair by nature to condemn anyone other than Halburton for her plight.

"It shouldn't be too hard for you to find another job here in Atlanta, Rebecca," Jonathan said, softening his stance to perch on the corner of her desk and place a large, gentle hand on the sleeve of her red blazer. "You're a good lawyer."

"I sent out résumés when Halburton started talking about working with Ballenger," Rebecca said, sinking into her swivel chair. "But it's too soon to get any responses. I start my vacation Wednesday, but ... I canceled my trip to England to stay in town and look for something—"

"Why wait until Wednesday?" Jonathan interrupted. "You've cleared all your work to take your two weeks of vacation. Do you have anything important to hold you here?"

"No." Rebecca shook her head.

Jonathan's intense expression demanded her attention. "Rebecca, you're an intelligent, determined young woman. George hired you to handle the legal problems of our expansion because he saw great potential in you. I think—if you'll permit me to express an opinion—that you've lost touch with yourself somewhere in the past two years. You're smart enough to learn from your experiences here. Instead of attacking the problem of finding a new position right now, why not get away for a few days? Can you go home and relax for a while?"

Rebecca sighed. "I'd just go crazy in my apartment."

"I mean *home*, Rebecca. Hometown. Family."

"Oh!" The image and sensation of the serenity and comfort of her hometown in rural central Georgia flashed into her mind. "Yes. That might be a good idea."

"Wrap up what's on your desk, and I'll clear it with George for you."

"*Jonathan*—" Her voice sounded more strident than she had expected, and she immediately got control of herself. "Jonathan—"

"Rebecca, you're a good person. Don't let a little misfortune sour you on the rest of the world." He bent down and kissed her on the cheek, like a big brother or a loving uncle. It only made her feel worse.

"You're right." Rebecca sighed and pressed her hands together, somehow deriving a surge of strength and energy from the gesture. "Maybe going home is the best thing to do, before I get started on applications and interviews."

"Have a nice vacation," Jonathan said, one hand on the doorknob. "See you in a few weeks."

Jonathan left the office, and Rebecca sat staring at the letter that had been in the envelope without trying to make any sense of it. With a gesture of finality, she put it back in the envelope and slipped it into her briefcase. Then she swept all the work on her desk into one neat pile and dumped it into her In basket.

Melda Hymes, her secretary, seemed confused when Rebecca locked her office door behind her and dropped the key on her desk. "See you in two weeks," she said. "If anyone needs me, I'll be at my family's home in Blakesley Hills. The number is in my file."

Two hours later she'd exchanged her skirt for slacks, thrown a few necessities into an overnight case and a carry-on bag, and closed up her apartment and was on her way through the rolling countryside of central Georgia. She was glad to get out of the heavy traffic bustling around Atlanta and its sprawling suburbs.

The hour-long drive was giving her too much time to think. But it was all water under the bridge, Rebecca thought, easing her foot onto the accelerator to climb yet another hill.

But maybe Jonathan was right. Maybe distance would give her a better perspective.

As she passed the sign that read Blakesley Hills City Limits, Rebecca took a deep breath and slowed the car slightly. It wouldn't do her morale any good to be hauled in for speeding in her hometown.

The broad lawns, majestic oak trees and rampant flower gardens of one of the oldest neighborhoods in town gave way to the edge of the commercial district, heralded by the Kerry County Junior High School she remembered attending. With a sense of shock, she noticed that the statue of General Blakesley, for whom the town was named, had been painted a ghastly purple, and that graffiti was smeared across the red brick wall of the recent addition to the school.

By now, though, she was driving through the main business blocks, where cars were parked diagonally by parking meters that supported pots of petunias and asparagus ferns. Part of her mother's handiwork, she recalled, as chairman of the Blakesley Hills Beautification Project.

The one traffic light in town stopped her just across from the red brick and marble Kerry County Courthouse. Looking up at the second floor, Rebecca saw that the lights were on in her father's office.

Deciding to stop in and surprise him, Rebecca began looking for a parking space. It would delay going home for a few more minutes, and facing her mother, the woman who could read her like a book. She could keep things from Big Ted Hobbs, but not from Margaret.

The hot August sun hit her as soon as she stepped out of the air-conditioned car. She strode across the street and up the traffic-hollowed marble steps to the double doors of the courthouse. An old man coming out held the door for her and tipped his hat when she thanked him. Socially, Blakesley Hills was at least fifty years behind Atlanta.

The first-floor corridor of the courthouse had the institutional atmosphere of hushed formality and muffled activity. Rebecca followed the permanent temporary sign that directed her to the elevator. She gripped the brass railing until the car shuddered and stopped on the second floor.

Once she stepped through the open office door, which was labeled in gold leaf letters Theodore E. Hobbs, Judge, Rebecca was greeted by Alice Grimm, his receptionist-secretary, whom Rebecca had known all her life.

"Is Daddy in?" Rebecca asked.

"Why, Rebecca! Sure he's in for you," Alice cooed softly, motioning toward the inner office.

Big Ted Hobbs was standing at his bookcase leafing through a law book when Rebecca slipped behind him and covered his eyes with her slim hands.

"Guess who?" she said.

"Rebecca!" he exclaimed, turning around to catch her in his arms, the law book still in his hand. "I thought you were on your way to England."

"No, I decided to come home instead," Rebecca said, accepting a kiss on the cheek.

"Well, let me take a look at you." He held her at arm's length and frowned. "You look like you need a vacation."

"I sure do." She was about to blurt out her dilemma to his understanding ear when the telephone on his desk buzzed.

"Excuse me, honey—" he said, lifting the receiver.

Rebecca couldn't help but notice the opened letter on her father's mahogany desk. First of all, it had the United States Justice Department seal on it, and the words *Federal Court of Appeals* and *appointment* jumped out at her. She took a deep breath and gripped the side of the desk for support as she dealt with the thrill of knowing that her father's long-held dream of sitting on the federal bench was possibly within his grasp.

"Why, that's fine, Frank," Big Ted Hobbs was drawling into the phone. "If you can't make the appointment this afternoon, I think it would be best if you stopped by the house this evening—around seven-thirty. I have my heart set on watching the Braves play the Dodgers on television tonight at eight, so don't keep me waiting," he said with humor.

Rebecca shook her head and clucked her tongue, mocking her father. "Still planning your life around the baseball games on television, Daddy?" she asked when he'd hung up.

"Well, if Frank isn't coming by this afternoon, I can get out of here early for a change!" Big Ted grinned, showing deep dimples in his attractively aging face. "The more time to spend with you."

"Your Honor?" Alice interrupted from the doorway. "You're due in court to hear that motion for continuance—"

Big Ted reached for his black judicial robes. "You go on home, Rebecca. I'll be along as soon as I can."

Rebecca's smile covered her disappointment at being shifted out of the office and having no recourse but to go home and face her mother. She strolled down the broad slate steps to the lobby, trailing her fingers lightly on the polished oak banister. Then the smile on her face grew more genuine.

She was home. In her car again, she turned at the Community Episcopal Church, slowing down to notice that the grounds were more neatly kept than in years past. She'd heard that Reverend Higgins had been reassigned, so a new minister must be in charge.

A block away, she noticed a man and two half-grown boys shoring up the rose trellis on Mrs. Jenkins's verandah. She didn't recognize them. The man, shirtless in the unrelenting August sun, was tanned a deep brown above his worn blue jeans. Although the boys seemed to be arguing with him, he appeared to be well in charge of the situation, banging away effortlessly with a hammer, the muscles of his broad shoulders and upper arms rippling smoothly with each stroke.

As he turned to say something to one of the boys, she got the full effect of the chiseled profile beneath his thatch of jet-black hair. The firm line of his chin, the straight prominence of his nose, were beyond attractive.

She raised an eyebrow and drove on. Anyone that handsome had to be spoken for in a town the size of Blakesley Hills. One of the main drawbacks of living in a small town was the scarcity of marriageable men.

Rebecca sighed. In many ways, Blakesley Hills was a long way from Atlanta!

Turning again, she rolled to a stop in front of her family's home, an old red brick, late-Victorian pile of a house that sat in the center of a broad, well-groomed lawn. On the veranda stood four matching rocking chairs, their paint this year a bright yellow that echoed the tiny marigolds in the round terra-cotta pots that accented each wooden step and the sidelights of the broad front door.

Her mother wasn't home, but as soon as she'd wrestled her bags into the front hall and dropped them on the polished oak floor that skimmed around the Oriental rugs she heard a car in the driveway. Her mother, who'd probably noticed her car parked in front of the house, called her name.

"Rebecca, honey! I thought you were going to England!" she called as she got out of Erma Hemple's car.

"Change of plans," Rebecca responded as she bounded down the steps on her way to close the trunk of her car, trying for a cheerful, unconcerned tone in front of her mother's longtime friend. "Hello, Mrs. Hemple."

Margaret Hobbs's brown eyes studied her daughter for an instant, then she turned to Erma. "I'll call you tomorrow about the quilt show program once I've talked to Mary."

Erma eased her car into reverse and waved as she backed out of the drive.

Margaret put her arm around her daughter's shoulders and started walking toward the house. "Well, now, what's the problem?"

There was no sense in putting it off. "Mama, I lost my job after working out Mr. Halburton's merger. The other company's staff counsel has more experience than I do," Rebecca said, comforted by her mother's arm as it rested on her shoulders.

"Well, it can't be all bad," her mother said in a more cheerful voice, dropping her purse on the table that held the telephone. "Have you had lunch?"

"No, but I'm not hungry."

Margaret looked deceptively preoccupied with searching for something in her personal appointment book. "I could stand some iced tea," she said at last, starting toward the kitchen. "How about you?"

"Yes, I'm parched."

They were sitting at the round table on the back porch, drinking from tall glasses of iced tea, sharing a plate of tuna sandwiches, when Margaret Hobbs surveyed her daughter with a knowing look.

Uncomfortable, Rebecca looked away from her mother, toward the old two-story carriage house, which was now a garage and storage attic. Life had been so simple when she'd been a child here, playing house in the old carriage house, making ladies' cotillions out of hollyhock and hibiscus blossoms. Back then, it had never entered her mind that ladies needed men to dance with, to escort them to the balls she staged. Boys and men had been a later discovery.

"How long can you stay?" her mother asked.

Rebecca shrugged. "Until I get my head on straight, I suppose."

Her mother laughed. "Then don't unpack too much, dear. You're one of the most levelheaded young women I've ever known."

Margaret calmly poured them both more tea from the glass pitcher on the table. "I'm sure losing your job had nothing to do with you as you. Just . . . karma."

Rebecca chuckled to herself. Mama was always a surprise. Oriental philosophies were rarely discussed in rural Georgia, but who was to say they weren't in force just the same?

Margaret seemed unconcerned, except for Rebecca's hurt feelings. Even sitting on her own back porch sipping iced tea, Margaret was an elegant woman. Her pale blond hair was swept into deep waves and held high off her neck with a gold comb. Her pink silk blouse looked as neat as when she'd put it on that morning, and her white wrapped skirt was uncreased by whatever she'd been doing.

Unlike other mothers, Margaret wasn't constantly asking her daughter when she was going to get married and settle down to keeping house and raising children. Somehow she conveyed the confidence that Rebecca would accomplish what she wanted to at the right time.

After all, Rebecca wasn't the only child in the Hobbs family. Her younger brother, Don, was off in Washington working as an aide to the congressman from the local district, and he was enough to worry about all by himself. But Margaret always had the unshakable faith that good things happened to those who waited. So she waited.

"I stopped by to see Daddy on my way," Rebecca said. "He thinks he'll be home early this afternoon."

"Oh, good! He's been working so hard lately, trying to get everything cleared away and caught up. There was quite a backlog of cases late this spring, for some reason, and he's just now getting around to some of them. Well, I'd better make more tea," Margaret said. "Why don't you go put on something cooler? You look so uncomfortable."

As usual, her mother was right. Rebecca went up the back stairs that curled between the kitchen and the back parlor and led her to the upper hall, just across from her old bedroom. In the dresser she found an old pair of white shorts and the top of a red bikini that had long since been orphaned.

Her complexion usually tanned without any problems, but for good measure she snatched up a cotton camp shirt to throw on when the sun got too hot.

She glanced into the mirror above the dresser, surprised that she looked better than she felt. Her dark brown hair was cut short to take advantage of its natural waves; the stylist she went to in Atlanta charged her an outrageous fee, but the results were always worth it. Mascara still accented her thick lashes, and a bit of lipstick remained on her full mouth. But the spark was gone.

She'd never had any difficulty with her looks, not until she'd realized that her attractiveness worked against her when she tried to be taken seriously intellectually. At first, when she'd finished law school and passed the Georgia bar exam, she hadn't been able to find a position in a law firm. Then she'd dressed down, and she'd finally settled for the position at Halburton Development, feeling she would be relegated to sitting behind a desk, poring over contracts and ledgers. But then she'd met Jonathan Douglas and decided to launch a two-pronged attack—making herself indispensable to the firm and attractive to Jonathan Douglas.

Rebecca shook her head at how far awry her plans had gone. Funny, she'd always thought Jonathan was so handsome. Now, as she pictured him in her mind, she remembered only his flaws. A receding hairline, a scar high on one cheek, a nose that had been broken at least once, maybe twice. His cleverness had attracted her, and it was probably that same cleverness that kept him aloof and watching for a woman who could do more for his career than Rebecca herself could. She'd never let it be known that she was the daughter of a circuit judge. Now Daddy had a chance to be a federal judge. Well, she didn't want a man if that made a difference to him.

There was just no way to win in this world, despite her mother's quiet confidence to the contrary.

Barefoot, Rebecca slipped down the back stairs again and fetched a beach towel from the lower cabinet in the pantry, where her mother always kept the picnic hamper and other gear ready for impromptu excursions. Margaret was a Scorpio with Sagittarius rising, always ready to go at a moment's notice, whether for romance or adventure.

The cool grass in the backyard prickled her feet as she crossed the lawn to a sunny place near the garage and spread out her towel. Sighing, Rebecca lay down on her back and looked up at the clear blue sky above the oak tree she'd climbed as a child.

Maybe Jonathan had known what he was talking about when he'd recommended that she come home and look at things the way she had when she'd been younger. It had been a long time since she'd taken the time to look up at the sky and contemplate infinity.

The sun warmed her quickly, and she turned on to her stomach, just as her father drove his sleek black sedan onto the brick apron in front of the garage.

"It sure didn't take you long to get into the spirit of vacation!" Big Ted said with a chuckle, pulling his lumpy briefcase from the passenger seat and slamming the door after him. "But I really thought you had your heart set on England."

"I'm changing jobs," she told him, deciding that he would learn about her personal catastrophe soon enough anyway. She might as well get it out in the open. "I thought it was best to save my money."

"Changing jobs?" Big Ted asked, stopping in his tracks. "I thought there were important things afoot at Halburton."

"There are, but—well...they merged with another firm that had a more experienced lawyer on staff. I was asked to step aside." Rebecca waited for his reaction, expecting outrage, or at least disappointment.

"Tough break, Becca. But I thought that job must be pretty dull for you anyway," Big Ted said with less concern than she'd expected. He loosened his somber dark tie. "You were made for courtrooms and paneled offices."

"Hey, I used to think so!" Rebecca laughed, squirming around to sit with her slender arms circling her knees. She looked toward the house, tilted her head and lowered her voice. "And what are you made for? I saw a very interesting letter on your desk while I was in your office. Does Mama know you're being considered for the federal court?"

"Not yet," Big Ted said, a spark coming into his hazel eyes. "I don't want to get her hopes up. This is the first time it's happened, and I really can't see why I'm being considered, except that I've been active in some of the campaigns lately."

"Oh, Daddy, I know how you hate politics—"

"Well, sometimes there are candidates that I believe in. And an appointment would be convenient. I don't like having to be elected to a higher bench. Being appointed is neater."

"I thought you were satisfied here."

"I am, but there isn't much going on here I didn't see ten years ago. I...I want a challenge...before it's too late."

"Daddy! I've never heard you talk like this!"

Big Ted chuckled. "Mostly because I've never even thought the thoughts I've had since I got that letter. I just keep reading it over and over. It's very seductive, you know?"

"Oh, yes, I know. I'd be very proud for you."

Big Ted smiled down at her, almost blushing.

"And proud for Mama, too!" she added.

"Doesn't she deserve it?" Big Ted asked, pure pride in his voice. "She's been beside me each step of the way, listening to my problems, keeping my secrets, putting up with bad moods when I have tough decisions to make."

"If you're offered the position you'll take it, then?"

"Who wouldn't?" Ted asked. Then he shrugged. "But, as I say, it's my first time. It won't happen—"

"Ted?" Margaret called from the house. "I thought I heard you drive in...."

"I'll be right there, honey," Big Ted called back, then looked down at Rebecca again. "We'll talk later. Don't get too much sun."

"I think I've had about enough for now, anyway," Rebecca said, but she still sat on the towel, watching the way the breeze ruffled the white petunias and red salvia around the back porch.

While looking in that direction, she caught only the shortest glimpse of the profile of the driver of a battered white pickup truck carrying an assortment of ladders and yard tools in its open bed as it rumbled past the front of the house, followed by two boys on bicycles who were weaving back and forth playfully, then racing to keep up with the vehicle.

They were the same boys she'd seen working on the trellis over at Mrs. Jenkins's house. Towheaded and bare to the waist, they were like so many other youngsters, but she noticed that they were twins.

She couldn't remember any twins in town, but then, she'd been gone—Lordy, had she been out of touch that long?

Rebecca got to her feet, tugged her camp shirt on and knotted it at her waist, then picked up the towel and gave it a good shake. Throwing it over her arm, she strolled slowly into the house.

In the kitchen, the oven door slammed closed just as Rebecca put the towel on a hook in the laundry room, where it would be tomorrow, when she got more serious sun.

"Becca, we're eating a little early because your daddy has someone coming over to the house this evening and—"

"I know, Mama." Rebecca laughed. "The Braves are on television tonight. I'm just going to unpack and jump into the shower, and I'll be right down." And right hungry! she thought. Funny, she hadn't been hungry in ages.

Chapter Two

"Your peach cobbler is as good as ever, Mama," Rebecca said, helping to clear the dinner plates from the round table in the corner of the kitchen.

"Well, I've had plenty of practice making it over the years," Margaret Hobbs said, then laughed. "I don't think your father minds having it every so often, either."

"What can I do to help you?" Rebecca asked, looking around the kitchen.

"Nothing here, darlin'," Margaret said, opening the dishwasher. "But scoot into your father's study and bring out the flower arrangement on the mantel. I did it for a wedding in there Friday evening, so it's probably looking sorry by now. Hurry, before his caller comes—"

Discretion had always been one of her mother's abiding tenets. She was never caught in the act of doing anything—unless, of course, she wanted to be.

Rebecca lifted the vase full of wilted gladioli and dahlias from the carved oak mantel in the study and scooped up a

few fallen petals just as she heard a car pull into the driveway. To avoid meeting whoever was coming into the hallway, she slipped out the door that led to the back porch.
She'd just put the heavy vase on the table there, trying to
decide if any of the blossoms could be salvaged for a new
bouquet, when she heard voices coming from the front
hallway.

"Good evening, Your Honor," she heard a well-trained
baritone voice say. Her father laughed, obviously guiding
his caller from the front hall back to his study.

"Let's not get into titles, Frank. Just first names."

"That might take some getting used to, sir," the caller
said, with a laugh that was deep and unpretentious.

Rebecca picked up the vase and headed for the door on
the other side of the porch, which would take her through
the laundry room to the kitchen. "These flowers all look
pretty tired, Mama."

"Well, do what you think is best. I have some calls to
make," Margaret said, reaching for the phone on the wall.
"I've got to catch Mary before she goes to her bridge club,
and then call Erma. I was going to call her tomorrow, but
I'll be too busy." She looked at the flowers for a long moment. "Yes, they're hopeless."

"I could pick something to replace them," Rebecca offered, wanting something to do.

"Those dahlias over by the fence are about ready," Margaret said, pushing buttons on the telephone from memory.
By the time Rebecca returned to the kitchen, her mother was
off somewhere, probably having decided to make the calls
from the phone upstairs.

Rebecca set about arranging a bunch of bright dahlias in
the heavy crystal vase, cheerfully snipping stems and lower
leaves with kitchen scissors. She tossed the clippings into the
wastebasket, tidied up the counter, dried her hands and re-

garded the arrangement with a critical eye. Not bad, she decided.

She'd heard an occasional word from the study, but they hadn't formed any sort of pattern. There wasn't any light-hearted laughter, so she assumed the topic was very serious. She wasn't in the habit of eavesdropping on her father's conversations. What went on in the study was often privileged communication and not for her ears.

She was rearranging one pink dahlia blossom when her mother slipped down the back stairs and glanced at the vase approvingly as she reached into the cupboard for the good crystal glasses.

"Take some of the pralines from the tin there on the counter and put them on one of Grandma Painter's plates," she instructed as she poured iced tea into the glasses.

Rebecca smiled and raised an eyebrow. "A Havilland plate, Mama? Daddy's company must be important."

Margaret Hobbs just made a little noise and put the filled glasses on a tray. "You take this into the study, dear. I just remembered another call I have to make."

Rebecca managed to knock on the study door without spilling the tea. Funny how she knew in her head she could do that but the memory of one disaster when she'd been a child always made her wary.

"Rebecca, dear," her father said when he opened the door, "I want you to meet someone."

Rebecca was dubious about meeting anyone at the moment. Her short brown hair was always in place—it was too short to get disarranged—and her complexion didn't need much in the way of makeup. But at the moment she felt defenseless, as though anyone could see right through her, could see how defeated she felt inside.

On the other hand, one didn't ignore one's father. He was a judge, after all, and he expected polite compliance with his wishes, even at home.

And what could be so bad about taking a deep breath and walking into the study?

Big Ted took the tray from her and placed it on the coffee table in the center of the room. His expression was doting, as always. "Rebecca, I want you to meet Frank Andrews."

The man was sitting with his back toward the door in the high-backed leather chair, only his dark hair visible. Still she couldn't help but recognize that barely trained crown as the one she'd been impressed with on the way home earlier that day. A prickle of anticipation ran through Rebecca.

She knew what he looked like without his shirt, his tanned shoulders gleaming under a sheen of perspiration in the August sun, jeans slung below a trim waist and outlining long, straight legs. She bit her lips together for a little color like the Southern belles of old and straightened her shoulders.

Frank Andrews stood up slowly, turning his classic profile toward her. He had an intelligent brow, straight black eyebrows above dark eyes, a regular nose that made a no-nonsense statement and a mouth that pushed deep slashes into his cheeks when he smiled.

And then she saw the stiff, round white collar above his black broadcloth tunic. It almost glowed in contrast to his tanned face.

For the briefest instant she looked up at him in stunned confusion, then composed her face into a gracious smile. It must have worked; the minister didn't laugh in her face.

"Frank's the new pastor at Community Church," Big Ted said. "He's taking on a special project for me."

She would have known he was a man of the cloth, even without the collar, just by the glow in his dark eyes. An indescribable something told her that he was set apart from lesser men. That look was intimidating—and Rebecca Hobbs wasn't often intimidated.

As an automatic reflex, Rebecca reached for his hand, accustomed to the big-city way of greeting associates and professionals. The hand that engulfed hers was strong and, surprisingly, callused.

"Miss Hobbs," he said, his voice soft and deep, enveloping her with a warmth that the summer evening had no need of. "It's nice to meet you."

"Reverend Andrews," Rebecca said tentatively.

"Please call me Frank. His Honor insists." He winked at her father and released her hand.

Big Ted slipped a praline from the plate on the coffee table and started around his desk.

"Sit down, Rebecca," her father said, indicating the other chair.

"I'd guess you've been in town less than two months," Rebecca said, more to her father than to the minister, as she sat down. "Long enough to get involved in one of his projects, but not long enough to learn how to avoid him."

Both Big Ted and Frank laughed. "Quite right," Frank said. "I came to Blakesley Hills in late June."

"It's rather quiet here, isn't it?" Rebecca asked.

"I like it, though," Frank said.

"Are you from a small town?" Rebecca asked.

"No. But it has about the same pace as where I went to seminary."

"To say nothing of everyone knowing everyone else's business." Rebecca laughed. "Believe me, the anonymity of a big city is sometimes comforting."

Big Ted turned to Frank. "Before Rebecca took a position as staff counsel with a development firm in Atlanta, she was involved in a youth advocacy program." He turned to Rebecca. "I want to pick your brain about something. What have you observed about the way juvenile troublemakers have been handled in Atlanta?"

"Sorry, Daddy," Rebecca sighed and crossed her legs, careful that her red cotton skirt covered her knees. "I've been too busy with real estate law and contracts to go looking at other areas of the legal system."

"Well, maybe you can help us anyway," Big Ted sighed, settling into the chair behind his desk and picking up his letter opener, an idle habit he had. "One night a few weeks ago, when I was out jogging, I caught the Blakesley twins painting the statue of General Blakesley. As a favor to the town's most prominent family, I decided to handle the situation outside the usual channels of the court. I'd just met Frank, and I thought we could straighten them out, helping each other in the process. Frank needed someone to help him with his new handyman business, and I thought the boys could do with some strong, positive male influence."

"Forgive me," Rebecca interrupted, "but I can't place any twins in the Blakesley family."

"Their father hasn't lived in Blakesley Hills since he was a kid," Big Ted explained. "He was sent to a military prep school when he was about fourteen, and from there he went to the Air Force Academy. Now he's retired after thirty years in the air force and runs a defense consulting business from here."

"These are the boys I saw working at Mrs. Jenkins's house this afternoon, then?" Rebecca asked, and she was answered with confirming nods. "They seem pretty lively."

Frank chuckled and crossed one polished black oxford over the other. There were signs of physical fatigue in the posture of his shoulders and the dark smudges under his eyes, but the glint in his eyes showed his mental alertness and involvement. "They keep me on my toes, that's for sure."

Masking her fascination with each small movement the young minister made, Rebecca looked from Frank to her father and then back again. She smiled and said, "Reverend Andrews—Frank—I wish I'd been around to warn you not to get involved with Daddy's special projects. He's been trying to keep every youngster in the county on the straight and narrow ever since I can remember. He still has the idealistic view that there's untapped good in everyone. Obviously he feels all the boys need is a little of yours to rub off on them to make them model citizens."

Frank Andrews chuckled, his smile showing more than straight white teeth. There was a certain appreciation of her wit—at the very least—that warmed more color into Rebecca's cheeks than the summer sun had.

"Well, the process is taking much more time and energy and forbearance than we anticipated," Frank said, his mood changing from light and bantering to serious.

"Unfortunately, the boys need more time than he has to give," Big Ted said. "They're about three years ahead of their peers academically, and light-years ahead in sophistication—much to our chagrin."

She studied Frank's dark eyes for a moment, trying to discount the interest she saw there as something impersonal, something owing to the topic of discussion, not to her own appearance. Even so, she had to moisten her lips and swallow before she spoke again.

"First of all, I doubt that giving a fresh coat of paint to the founder's statue would even have raised an eyebrow in Atlanta," she said. "I find it puzzling they'd do such a thing to their—what? Great-grandfather?"

"Great-great-grandfather," Big Ted responded.

"They won't talk about it," Frank said, spreading his broad hands in a helpless gesture. "They change the subject. And speaking about talking! They routinely express themselves in such violent language, I'm appalled."

"Maybe they're just trying to shock you," Rebecca suggested. "They're looking for a reaction."

"I think they get enough of a reaction from their father and stepmother," Big Ted said, drawing circles on his blotter with his letter opener. "I've had long conversations with both of them, and they're at their wits' end, too. I'm wondering, Rebecca dear, if you'll help us out on this one."

"Daddy, what can I do?" Rebecca asked, interested yet reluctant to step into the issue. "I haven't been around juveniles since my law school days, when I worked with the youth advocacy program. And these boys are certainly not the type of kid I saw there."

"You at least had *that* experience," Big Ted said, his beaming smile telling her that no daughter of his could be less than wonderful at anything.

Rebecca acknowledged his faith in her. A glance at Frank Andrews, however, told her that he was as skeptical about her worth as she was. "I admire you both for trying to straighten out these boys before they get into real trouble, but by now, Daddy, you should know you can't save everybody."

"All I'm asking is that you give it some thought," Big Ted said.

"I'd run over to Milledgeville and read through the child psychology books over there," Frank said, a furrow of weariness crossing his forehead, "but I've got to do all the fix-up jobs I can get to keep body and soul together. Any reading time I have goes toward keeping parish books and preparing sermons."

Rebecca looked over at him, unaware of the sympathy in her eyes. "All right, I'll give it some thought." Rebecca stressed the last word, promising nothing more. She got to her feet slowly and reached for Frank's hand as he stood up. "It's been nice meeting you, Reverend Andrews."

"Will you be staying in town long?" Frank asked, taking her hand and holding it a bit longer than she expected.

The prospect of spending her whole vacation here was becoming increasingly attractive. "I just may stay more than a few days," she conceded, aware that she was flirting with him ever so slightly and ashamed of herself for it.

He has the most startling eyes, Rebecca thought to herself as she studied his face in the mixture of twilight and soft lamplight. *For a man of God, he's got the very devil in his eyes.*

She couldn't get away from the study quickly enough. Red faced and confused at being physically attracted to a man of the cloth after such a brief first meeting, she escaped to the back parlor and stood flipping through the channels on the television, barely conscious of what she was looking for.

She passed the baseball game and had to go back to it. Then she kicked off her sandals and sank down on the chintz-covered wicker settee, tucking her feet up under her and hugging a throw pillow to her chest.

As far as Rebecca was concerned, dark-haired men were dangerous. Frank Andrews looked as though he could easily have been a rough and reckless motorcycle rider or a cutthroat big-city entrepreneur. Clerical black made him no less devastating to the well-ordered resolve she'd made to be involved only with "safe" men, men who were predictable, not a threat to her hard won independence—and boring. Frank was none of the above, an enigma.

She pounded her fist into the pillow she was holding. The scowl on her face reflected the dark thoughts she was entertaining. What good would coming home do her if all she thought about was the disappointment of losing her job in Atlanta? She dreaded going back. Nor did she want to get involved with one of her father's special projects, even though the man already involved in said project was stunningly attractive.

Her father came into the back parlor, glanced at the television screen and dropped a manila file on the cushion beside her. "That's what I have on the Blakesley boys," he told her.

Well, she didn't have anything else to do but sit there and brood about herself, Rebecca thought, opening the file where it lay and glancing at the first page. Her father's handwriting hadn't improved over the years. It was a challenge to decipher at first, but once she got used to seeing it again she figured out the important facts.

The boys, Timothy Titus Blakesley and James Joseph Blakesley, were thirteen years old, the sons of a career air force officer who'd lately been posted to overseas bases and had brought his sons with him. Their mother had died when they were nine, and their father had recently remarried.

Rebecca shook her head. The story she wove around the bare facts was one of isolation and too many changes in the boys' short lives. No wonder they were making other people miserable. They were probably, in some ways, pretty miserable themselves.

"Popcorn?" Margaret asked from the kitchen door. "Beer? Get yer soft drinks he-ah!"

Rebecca laughed in spite of herself, snatching a pile of magazines off the coffee table as her mother approached with a tray of snacks.

"What's that you're reading?" Margaret asked, sitting down beside Rebecca.

Rebecca looked at her father. "Privileged?"

"Nah," her father said, digging into his bowl of popcorn. "Your mother knows about it. Who do you think suggested I ask Frank to help?"

Rebecca nodded her head and chuckled. "I should have known."

"Did you meet Frank?" her mother asked with deceptive simplicity.

Rebecca nodded. Surely her mother wasn't matchmaking. Frank Andrews was attractive, but— No, Margaret wouldn't . . .

"He's in a difficult position," Margaret explained, settling herself to enjoy her bowl of popcorn. "The church can't afford to pay him more than a pittance. He's just back from missionary duty and is adjusting to being back in the States. I guess he's having as hard a time getting used to us as we are to him."

Margaret put aside her popcorn, wiped her hands on a napkin and picked up her needlework basket. One eye on the television, she began to rummage through the basket, taking out scissors and scraps of brightly colored fabric.

"What are you making?" Rebecca asked, not ready to pursue any more information about Frank Andrews.

"Oh, I'm not making this. It's a quilt the women of the church are making to raffle off," Margaret explained. "Since, unlike your Aunt Ruth, I don't quilt, I'm stuck with cutting out these endless triangles!"

Rebecca laughed, picturing how Aunt Ruth would have talked the women of Community Church into making the quilt, deciding who should do what to contribute to the project. Margaret, whose talents leaned more toward flower arranging, organizing socials and baking, would be relegated to cutting out tiny pieces of fabric for someone else to sew together.

"Well, it doesn't look that hard," Rebecca said. "Do you have another pair of scissors?"

"Hush!" her father growled from his easy chair on the other side of the room. "We've got two on base and no one out!"

Margaret gave her daughter a knowing look. "Yes, dear. We'll try not to make too much noise."

Even the ceiling fan going at its highest setting didn't make Rebecca's bedroom any more comfortable in the hot, muggy August night. The ruffles of the sheer priscilla curtains hung limp, their fibers glistening in the light from the streetlamp at the corner.

She just couldn't sleep.

Disregarding the short nightshirt that covered very little of her, she slipped downstairs to the back parlor and retrieved the Blakesley twins' file from the end table where she'd left it.

What did her father expect her to do that could help Frank Andrews understand the boys and work some miracle of social salvation? she wondered.

Stretching out on her bed again, she adjusted the bedside lamp so that she could read the file. There was nothing there that she hadn't seen before.

She tried to think back to some "service brats" she'd known, particularly in college. The three fellows she'd met in prelaw had all been well-grounded in the classics, mathematics and sciences, but they had all lacked a sense of social foundation, of roots, aside from their immediate families.

What an awful way to be at such a vulnerable age as thirteen! she thought with sudden insight. She thought of the boys she'd known at that age; not quite ready for an interest in girls, perhaps, but starting to strut about in macho poses. In addition, the only people the Blakesley twins seemed to have been able to depend upon were each other.

That observation struck her as a significant thought. Frantically she searched the nightstand drawer for a pencil, wanting to write it down before she lost the idea. She had to write carefully, with only a paperback novel as a desk. Maybe the cause of the Blakesley boys' troublemaking streak had as much to do with being twins as with being service brats. She was almost certain the loss of their mother and the acquisition of their new stepmother had only added to the problem.

Something bothered Rebecca about the situation. She tried for a long moment to bring the thought to the surface, but after a few fruitless moments she closed the file and put it aside. Dispirited, she turned out the lamp and laid her head on her pillow, sat up again and turned the pillow over so that it would be cooler against her cheek.

Unbidden, the memory of Frank Andrews's dark eyes floated before her. He certainly was a handsome man, rare as hens' teeth in such a small town. Which would mean that his stay would probably be short, though not unnoticed by every unmarried woman between the ages of fourteen and eighty-four.

And he'd probably blithely ignore them all, unless he found someone who was totally innocent of worldly contamination, a self-effacing wallflower—plain as dishwater and willing to settle for four kids, semiannual uprootings and the burden of running the Sunday school, the flower committee and the women's missionary circle.

Knowing she fit none of those criteria, Rebecca frowned in the darkness.

Her legal training had taught her not to jump to such conclusions, but now, in the muggy darkness, with crickets chirping and the ceiling fan humming monotonously overhead, she indulged her imagination. She should be above the vague feeling of disappointment she'd experienced when she'd seen the round white collar he wore. But she couldn't get past the thought of the collar being a barrier to any relationship between them.

And why was she expecting a relationship?

Because when she had first seen Frank Andrews, hammering away at Mrs. Jenkins's rose trellis, she'd felt a stirring inside, an undeniable attraction. It wasn't a completely new feeling to Rebecca, but she'd never felt it as strongly as today.

But mostly Rebecca felt anger at herself. She was forever leaping three steps ahead of reality in her imagination.

By no stretch of the imagination could she think of herself as a wallflower. She'd always been the first or second girl asked to any school dance, and she'd never been at a loss for male companionship on a Saturday night. She'd never done anything truly scandalous—at least nothing that she now viewed with any great horror. But she still wouldn't be the right woman for a man like Frank Andrews. The idea was ridiculous, and what was even more so was that a part of her wished she were.

She pounded her pillow and vowed to fall asleep. Someone had told her once that she could tell how hot the air outside was if she could isolate the sound of one cricket chirping and count the chirps it made in one minute. She fell asleep counting, having given up faith in the nature lore as she remembered it.

But her fitful sleep was punctuated by troubled dreams, dreams of a man with eyes that glowed with a missionary's zeal at one moment and with a rogue's passion the next.

* * *

"Oh! You startled me," Margaret said, turning from the sink where she was filling the coffeepot to see Rebecca in the kitchen doorway. "Did you sleep well?"

"No," Rebecca said miserably, padding across the cool tile floor in her bare feet and dropping the Blakesley file at her accustomed place at the breakfast table.

"Maybe tonight you should sleep on the upstairs porch," Margaret suggested.

Rebecca grimaced at the thought of doing something that in her childhood had been a treat she looked forward to every spring. Now all she thought of were the bugs and moths. She shuddered and reached for the morning paper. In the upper corner there was a little picture with the sun peeking from behind a cloud and an umbrella hiding part of the moon.

"It's going to rain tonight," she mumbled.

"You're still lousy company in the morning," Margaret said cheerfully, sliding the glass coffeepot onto the platform of the coffee maker.

"Sorry," Rebecca apologized, glancing at the headlines. She would make the effort to match her mother's spirit. Starting tomorrow.

"Morning, darlin'. Rebecca, honey," Big Ted said, coming into the kitchen, wearing a red running suit after his morning jog around the block. He kissed each of them in turn. "I see you're working on my project for me," he said to Rebecca as he lowered himself to his chair and picked up the glass of tomato juice that was sitting there.

"Um," Rebecca responded.

"I think it kept her awake last night," Margaret informed him.

"Ah, I didn't mean you had to solve the problem all at once," Big Ted said.

"I couldn't sleep in the first place," Rebecca told him. "I just thought I'd put the time to good use."

"Well, did you come up with anything?" her father asked.

"Probably not." Rebecca sighed. "You know how it is. You have a brilliant idea in the middle of the night, but in the light of day it just doesn't make sense."

"So what are you going to do with your day?" Big Ted asked her.

At the moment, going back to bed held a certain attraction, but Rebecca knew she didn't have a chance.

"I have a meeting of the restoration society at the library at a quarter past nine," Margaret told her, taking a cantaloupe from the refrigerator. "You're welcome to ride over with me. At eleven I have a meeting of the fall festival committee at the church, and I have to drop by at Ruth's after that. Then, this afternoon, I'm taking Ruth to a meeting over at Erma's about the quilt project."

"Mother!" Rebecca laughed in mock horror. "I didn't get much sleep last night, and you wear me out just telling me your schedule!"

"Well, it's Tuesday..." Margaret said cryptically.

"I thought you might like to come over to the courthouse and watch an interesting civil case that's scheduled today," Big Ted said.

"I've got a date with a paperback novel," Rebecca said, patting the cover of the book she'd found in her room the night before. "Then I'm going to get some sun before it rains."

"Whatever you say." Big Ted smiled, then finished his tomato juice.

"Then you don't want to come to the meetings with me?" Margaret said, a thinly veiled message in her voice.

Rebecca looked up at her mother, and the discussions they'd had when she'd been a girl played in her head. She couldn't turn her mother down without being thought rude. Well, it would be all over town by now that she was home, and she might as well put in an appearance, for her mother's sake.

"No, I'll come," she said.

"I'm glad you decided to come with me this morning," Margaret said when Big Ted had left the table to dress for work. "I was afraid I was going to have to pull rank on you." She poured herself a little more coffee. "I don't want you to sit around here moping, and I don't particularly like giving lectures on how much you have going for you."

"I'll consider myself lectured, Mama," Rebecca said, smiling wryly at her mother. "Actually, I do rather look forward to a little quiet browse through the library this morning. I guess I've been in a rut, writing all those construction and merger contracts. Sort of...out of touch with real people."

Her mother made a little sound in her throat, but Rebecca couldn't quite decipher its meaning.

Chapter Three

The library had been built in the thirties, but it was supposed to look older—Greek Classic Revival. The walls of the reading rooms were an ancient green, which added to the effect.

Rebecca noted that hardly anything had changed over the years she'd been away from home. She wandered through the long rows of bookshelves, trying to find old favorites, only to be dismayed that the system of cataloging had been updated.

But she found some slick photographic books about England and decided that if she couldn't tramp through the streets of London in person she could at least glance at pictures of what she was missing. While she slowly turned from one magnificent photo to another, she was conscious of a spirited meeting behind the doors of the community room.

She overheard an angry discussion about one of the elderly women in Blakesley Hills being displaced from her lovely old house because she could no longer pay the taxes on it and a developer wanted the property for a shopping plaza.

As though Blakesley Hills needed a shopping plaza! Rebecca thought, shaking her head and going back to the task at hand.

When the meeting broke up—mostly because Margaret Hobbs wasn't the only woman there who was expected at Community Church for the meeting of the fall festival committee—Margaret brought Thelma Pettigrew over to the table where Rebecca was reading. "I promised Thelma a ride over to the church, dear," Margaret said. "Are you ready to leave?"

"Just about," Rebecca said, stacking the books she'd been reading. "I'll meet you outside at the car as soon as I return these."

Thelma had settled into the back seat of Margaret's roomy station wagon and was still fuming about the meeting. "Well, I'll tell you, it makes things awfully hard at home. I've asked Carl three times to take on Mrs. Gruber as a *pro bono* case, but he represents ERM Properties and says that it would be a conflict of interests. And Minnifield, Drake and Hobbs doesn't handle public-interest cases anymore. Which just leaves Peter Martin and Jim Cates."

Anyone who didn't know the law firms in town would have been baffled by Thelma's tirade, but Rebecca was fascinated.

"It's still Minnifield, Drake and Hobbs?" she asked. "After all these years?"

"Well, in name only," Margaret said. "Your father's no longer connected with the firm. I suppose they're just waiting for the old stationery to run out." She and Thelma laughed.

"What about Peter Martin?" Rebecca asked.

"He's mostly involved in criminal work and divorces," Thelma said, her distaste evident in her tone.

"Jim Cates?"

"Well . . . if we could afford him . . ."

"Rebecca, you could represent Mrs. Gruber." Margaret made the suggestion as though she'd just thought of it, but Rebecca suspected that this had been her plan all along.

"No, Mama," she said, trying to be gentle yet firm. "I'm only going to be here a few days. I'll probably go back to Atlanta later this week. I've got to—"

"Rebecca, that's an excellent idea!" Thelma said, as though she hadn't heard a word of the young woman's. "Why don't you just do a little digging? We'd love to be able to establish that house as a historical landmark. We just haven't had the time to find an angle. And I'm afraid ERM Properties is going to win this one just because they have the big bucks on their side."

"ERM Properties is going to say that the house is unsafe and ought to be condemned," Margaret said with a sigh. "They'll say that it would take too much to repair and maintain—"

"Well, I'll tell you, a little attention to the yard, maybe a coat of paint—" Thelma said.

"See, that's the problem!" Rebecca exclaimed. "It'll take more than the legal fees. It'll take hundreds of dollars."

Thelma was suddenly deflated. "That's a good point. The restoration society doesn't have a large treasury."

Margaret chuckled. "That's an understatement."

"What about time?" Rebecca asked. "Time is money. Can anyone give some time to help out Mrs. Gruber?"

"Well, I'm scheduled up to my eyes," Thelma said.

"So's Mama. . . ." Rebecca said unenthusiastically.

"Time is not something we have a lot of. Most of us are working on the church festival, and, given a choice, I'm

afraid most of us will say that the church is in greater need,"
Margaret said, parking the station wagon in the church lot.

The ladies in the church raised a clamor of greetings when
Rebecca walked into the cool, cavernous meeting hall. There
wasn't one in the dozen that Rebecca hadn't known all her
life.

"I thought you were going to England this summer," one
of them chirped after kissing Rebecca somewhere in the vicinity of her cheek.

"Well, the plans changed, Mrs. Cline," Rebecca said
slowly.

"Oh! Horace and I were to go on a cruise a few years ago
and—well, the company was just a fraud. We were two years
getting our money back from them, and then they went into
bankruptcy."

"It's nothing as distressing as that," Rebecca told her,
moving slowly toward a group of folding chairs to avoid
discussing her reasons for being home.

"Have you met our new minister?" Mrs. Thurston asked.

"Yes," Rebecca said. "Last night."

The ladies twittered about the attributes of the new pastor for a few minutes, and then Margaret called them to order.

Rebecca had to admit that her mother's methods of organization were truly impressive. She knew just how to
handle every problem any of the subcommittees had, who
could best handle what, where to find the cheapest supplies
and who would donate the things that were needed.

"It's too late to do that for this festival," Margaret said
in answer to one suggestion from the floor. "But we need to
raise so much money, it appears to me that we'll need to
have a Christmas bazaar, too. Rebecca, will you take a note
of Martha's suggestion, and we'll put it aside...."

It seemed that everyone had ideas for a Christmas bazaar, and they kept Rebecca busy jotting them down, whispering them to her with a watchful eye turned toward her mother so that they wouldn't disturb anyone else or miss anything that was being said. She looked at her mother and smiled to herself. This was what her mother did best—delegate responsibilities. She was absolutely incredible.

"Rebecca, it's too bad you won't be here for the fall festival," Mrs. Thurston said as the meeting broke up.

"It does sound like fun," Rebecca admitted. "Since it's on a Saturday, I just might be able to run down here for the day."

"Oh, I hope so," Mrs. Thurston said, and hurried to catch up with someone who was leaving the hall.

"Now," Margaret said, collecting her purse, "we have to go over to Ruth's for a few minutes."

"Are you going to head up the Christmas bazaar?" Rebecca asked her mother.

"I suppose so," Margaret said, with a little tilt to her head. "I don't know of anyone else who could."

On the short drive over to her Aunt Ruth's house, Rebecca read the suggestions for the bazaar to her mother, and Margaret added more of her own.

"How do you come up with these ideas?" Rebecca asked, struggling to jot them down as the station wagon traversed a street that was badly in need of repair.

"Go to other churches' bazaars," her mother said seriously. "Then improve on what they do."

Aunt Ruth was a shorter, slightly rounder version of her stylish sister, but Ruth had never had much inclination to be the social butterfly Margaret was by nature.

"Why, Rebecca!" her aunt exclaimed, hugging her happily. "I was so surprised to hear that you were home. When Frank came home last night—"

Rebecca's brow creased in confusion. "Frank?"

"Reverend Andrews," Ruth said, moving her sewing aside so that Rebecca could sit on the metal porch glider with her. "I offered to take him in as a boarder. He can walk to the church from here, and it's quiet when he needs to study. I thought, well, if it works out with him, after he leaves I might take other boarders. Joe's pension doesn't go very far for me, you know."

Just the way things happen in a small town, Rebecca thought. You meet someone and you start tripping over him every time you turn around.

Margaret was taking a plastic bag from her satchellike purse. "Rebecca and I cut out triangles last night until we were blue in the face," she said, handing them to Ruth.

"How do you think you will be at squares?" Ruth asked, reaching into her enormous, overflowing workbasket for more fabric.

Rebecca laughed and shook her head. She should have expected as much.

"Why, he's no trouble at all," Aunt Ruth exclaimed when Margaret asked how she'd been getting along with Reverend Andrews. "He doesn't talk much about himself, but he does come from a nice family. It shows in the little ways, you know."

She filled Rebecca in on Reverend Andrews' exploits as a missionary in Central America and his reluctant return to the States after bouts with tropical diseases. Having only recently accepted the assignment to the Blakesley Hills parish, he'd had neither the time nor the funds to set up his own household, so Ruth had taken him in and was making certain that he had adequate meals and a clean place to stay.

Rebecca smiled at the aptness of the selection. Aunt Ruth was a hoverer, a demon housekeeper and a cook of good hearty food, as evidenced by her three strapping sons, now all on their own. No doubt, staying with Aunt Ruth, Frank Andrews was also getting adequate background on the past fifty years of Blakesley Hills and its inhabitants. Aunt Ruth was discreet but knowledgeable.

"What happened to the parsonage?" Rebecca asked her mother when they'd returned to the car.

"The denomination has sold most of the parsonages," Margaret told her. "In some cases the parishes needed the money for other expansion. Often the houses were hopelessly outdated and in need of massive remodeling. It just makes better economic sense for ministers to own their own homes."

Rebecca, being familiar with real estate, could understand the economics involved. Plus, the arrangement gave Aunt Ruth someone to spoil, now that she was a widow and her three sons had all left home.

A few minutes later, Margaret settled herself behind the wheel of her station wagon and put the car in gear. "Of course, everyone in the parish is sending their light carpentry and yard work Frank's way to eke out his stipend from the church. He's quite good, I'm told. He helped rebuild a church and school damaged by an earthquake where he'd been stationed."

Such a paragon! Rebecca thought as she and her mother drove home. And such a burden for him to be in such a fishbowl existence, with the whole town watching his every move!

It certainly wasn't a life she would choose for herself.

Having begged off her mother's afternoon round of activities, Rebecca put the lunch dishes into the dishwasher and reached for the beachtowel she'd left in the laundry room. She might be able to get a little sun before the clouds got any thicker.

As it was, every few minutes a cloud blocked the sun, and Rebecca enjoyed the breeze that was blowing from the northwest. During one respite from the searing rays of the sun she noticed that a large part of the oak tree nearest the garage seemed to be losing its leaves. Strange. Well, if part of the tree was dying, it was no shame for the tree that had been there forever. She would tell her father about it and he'd take care of it. Somewhere a telephone was ringing, and by the time she realized it was her father's line in the study she was too slow to get it before the caller hung up.

She stared down at the phone for a moment. "I hope it wasn't important," she said to herself, starting toward the yard again. Then a thought brought her up short. "What if it was about his appointment to the federal bench?"

She closed the door that led from the study to the back porch and retrieved her towel. Maybe she'd better stay close to the phone to see if they would call again. Which meant spending some time in the study with her father's collection of leather-bound law books.

She might as well see what she could come up with to help Mrs. Gruber, if there was anything in the law.

"Historical significance..." she mused.

She sat thinking in her father's chair for a long while. Then she dialed his office number.

"Alice? This is Rebecca. About fifteen minutes ago there was a call that rang in on Daddy's private number, and the party hung up before I could answer it...."

"Not to worry," Alice said cheerfully. "The call was made to the office."

"Good. I won't sit here brooding anymore. I think I'll go out for a little while."

"You don't want to talk to His Honor?"

"Is he free?"

"He's on recess. I'll put you through."

"Daddy?"

"Yes, punkin'?"

"Can I ask you something?"

"Sure."

"It's about Mrs. Gruber's house. Does she have legal representation?"

"Not that I know of."

"Do you mind if I look into it?"

There was a silence at the other end of the line. "It's a free country," he said at last.

"Thanks. See you later."

Rebecca ran up the back stairs and dug out fresh clothes, then headed toward the bath to take a shower, legal thoughts tumbling through her mind.

As the family gathered for dinner in the kitchen, Rebecca was trying to ignore the whistling wind and pounding rain that had brought early darkness.

"I hope I haven't caused any trouble for you by going over to talk to Mrs. Gruber about her problem," Rebecca told her father.

"Now, Rebecca, as I told you, it's a free country. If you seriously feel you can help that dear woman, I have nothing to say about it," her father told her, cutting into his pork chop.

"Dad, I certainly didn't go over there thinking that I will ever make a penny on her case. I just don't want to see that house bulldozed for a shopping plaza when the town doesn't even need one. And, knowing how most developers work, I know they'd pay as little as they possibly could for the land and she'd get nothing out of it."

"Yes, yes, I can see that," Big Ted said with a sigh. "So, what did you decide to do about it?"

"I haven't decided much of anything," Rebecca said, cringing when another crack of thunder rumbled through the air, making the overhead lamp quiver slightly. "I went to talk to her about her house. That place has the most incredible turned woodwork."

"You know, back in the thirties and forties, you were a nobody if you didn't take piano lessons from Agnes Gruber," Margaret interjected. "Some of the least talented children in the county sat on her piano stool for an hour every week. Luckily, by the time I was old enough to take piano lessons my mother had discovered I had a singing voice, so I didn't have to go there. We all thought the Gruber house was creepy!"

Rebecca laughed. "I suppose half of you would give your eyeteeth to get hold of it now. I asked Mrs. Gruber if the place had any historical significance, and she said she didn't think so. Her father-in-law used to joke about having gotten the house mail-order from Sears Roebuck."

"That's a Sears house?" Margaret asked, wide-eyed. "You brilliant child!"

"What?" Rebecca asked as she put gravy on her rice.

"Well, granted, I'm new to the restoration society, and they asked me to join mostly because of my gardening background, but I saw an article in a magazine Thelma loaned me a few months ago about the Sears houses," Margaret said, beaming. "I'll call her—"

She was interrupted by a bright flash of pink light, a rumble and a sustained crash, followed by the sound of splintering wood and shattering glass.

"Good God, what was that?" Big Ted roared, already on his feet and gazing out the window. He turned on the backyard lights. "Lightning struck the oak tree and dumped it on the garage!"

"I was going to tell you part of that tree was dying," Rebecca said, following him to the window. "I'll run out and see if the cars are all right."

"Rebecca! Wait a minute!" her mother called after her.

But Rebecca had already grabbed an old umbrella and a flashlight from the laundry room and was heading toward the porch. Big Ted had reached for the telephone, and Margaret was searching for something.

A flash of lightning showed that the damage was confined to the roof and the attic. Rebecca hurried into the building using the small side door. She doubted the wisdom of using any of the three broad overhead doors, a thought that hadn't fully materialized but just given her a feeling that caution was wiser than brash reaction. She left the umbrella on a wide patch of cement floor in the work area, then turned to the cars. She gave them a cursory inspection with the flashlight and found them safe and secure. She turned to the stairs and climbed up into the darkness of the second floor.

A strong, wet gust of wind buffeted her at the top of the stairs. The part of the oak tree that had broken free lay on a bank of boxes and rafters and shingles it had brought down. There was now a gaping hole where the center window had been. Glass and shattered wood were everywhere.

Rebecca reached for the cord of the nearest overhead light, but though she yanked it several times, the light did not respond. Apparently the tree had taken out the electrical line, too.

The place was a mess! Rebecca turned off the flashlight to save the battery. She could see the problem as well as she wanted to in the orange glow of the streetlamp on the corner and the frequent flashes of lightning.

She was just about to trundle back downstairs to take a look at the ceiling under the breach in the wall when she heard a motor outside and a battered white pickup truck came to a halt on the garage apron, its headlights focused on the center of the building.

Big Ted came running from the house, wearing his heavy rain gear, complete with boots.

"Frank! Thanks for coming!" he yelled to the man getting out of the truck.

"You've got quite a mess here," Frank yelled over the roar of the storm.

"Let's get inside!" Big Ted found, as Rebecca had, that the electric lights didn't work.

"It's just as well," Frank said.

"Rebecca!" her father called to her.

"Up here, Daddy," she called back, shining the flashlight on the stairs so that they could see their way up. "The cars are all right. Most of the damage is up here."

Frank mopped rainwater from his face and surveyed the damage Rebecca's flashlight outlined. "The first thing to do is to get a tarpaulin over the hole there. Do you have one?"

"Yes, but not that big," Big Ted said.

"Neither is mine, but the two of them together might do the trick," Frank said, taking charge. "Then we'll chop up the tree so it doesn't block the doors of the garage. That's about all we can do tonight."

"Yes," Big Ted agreed. "The insurance adjuster can't come until tomorrow morning, but he promised he'd be early."

"Good! Let's get to work!" Frank rigged a lamp to his truck's battery so that they didn't have to rely on the flashlight, freeing Rebecca to be ordered around doing her share of the work. She didn't mind the broken thumbnail or the scraped ankle she acquired in the process of jettisoning the offending treetop before securing the tarpaulin. Intent on shoring up the battered garage as quickly as possible she was too busy to care how she looked. The raging storm was letting up slightly, but it still hampered their work.

Frank took a chain saw from the toolbox in his truck and attacked the heavy trunk of the tree in front of the garage doors. "Now for the fun part!" He laughed and got to work.

"Those logs are going to be too heavy for you to handle, Rebecca," her father said. "Why don't you go in the house and get out of those wet clothes? Ask your mother to make us a pot of coffee. We didn't finish our dinners, did we?"

"No, and I'm beginning to feel it." Rebecca replied.

Margaret, of course, needed no instructions. She'd made a fresh pot of coffee and put out fresh towels by the door of the laundry room.

"I brought a robe down for you," she called out from the kitchen. "Why don't you just get out of your wet things there and run up and take a bath?"

"Don't think I can run, Mama, but the rest of it sounds good," Rebecca said.

When she'd put on fresh slacks and shirt she returned to the kitchen, just as Big Ted and Frank stomped up onto the porch.

Margaret handed them towels before they'd even gotten through the laundry room door. "I have your dinners on the table," she said, a glint of humor in her eyes. "Again. Frank, there's a fresh running suit of Ted's in the back parlor, if you'd care to get out of your wet things."

He looked down at her gratefully and disappeared, closing the door behind him.

"Well, we'll have firewood this winter," Big Ted said, toweling off his face, then rubbing his white hair vigorously. "That coffee smells fantastic. Rebecca, you worked like a trooper out there. Thank you."

Rebecca shrugged her shoulders and took her place at the table. "What's it going to take to fix the garage up again?"

"I'm too hungry to think about it now," Ted said, sniffing at the tureen of homemade soup in the center of the table. Margaret always had containers of it in the freezer, ready for an unexpected event like this.

"Don't wait for me to change, Rebecca. I'll be back in a few minutes."

Rebecca looked at the food on the table and took a deep breath. Now that she'd come to a full stop, she was almost too tired to pick up a spoon.

"How bad is the damage?" Margaret asked, ladling soup into a bowl and placing it in front of her.

"The middle window and the roof over it—" Rebecca said.

"What about the cars?"

"They're fine," Rebecca told her. " A lot of things in the attic were either squashed or soaked."

Margaret ladled soup into another bowl and studied it to see if it was full enough. "That was mostly the outside Christmas decorations and things I'd put aside for yard sales, so it's no great loss."

Frank came into the kitchen wearing a royal blue running suit of Big Ted's, the zipper of the jacket closed only to the middle of his broad chest. He carried his own sodden clothes rolled up in his hand.

"Have you a bag I can put these in, Mrs. Hobbs?"

"Nonsense! Put them in on the washer and I'll run them with Ted and Rebecca's things. You can pick them up tomorrow. Sit down and eat something."

When he returned from the laundry room, Frank sat down across from Rebecca and surveyed the plate in front of him. "I'm in a bit of a quandary here," he said, looking up at Rebecca with a glimmer of mirth in his dark eyes. "I'd just said grace when Big Ted called, and I didn't get to eat anything. Should I say grace again?''

Rebecca looked back at him with what she hoped was a matching expression. ''Law, not theology, is my field of expertise. It couldn't hurt,'' she advised, ''but Mom's not that bad a cook.''

Frank chuckled to himself, broke eye contact with Rebecca—perhaps a bit reluctantly—and folded his hands in front of him. If he asked a blessing, he did it silently and very briefly.

Big Ted came into the room and seated himself in his usual place. ''So, Frank, how long do you think it will take you and the boys to patch up the garage?''

''Two days,'' Frank said. ''We'll get started just as soon as the insurance man sees it. I had some other jobs lined up tomorrow and the next day, but they're nothing I can't postpone.''

''I've been wondering, Frank,'' Rebecca said, ''how much it would take to clean up Mrs. Gruber's yard and make a few simple repairs. She's got a broken window, and one shutter is just hanging on one hinge.''

''I've often thought, when I drive past, what I'd do with that place,'' Frank told her. ''But it would take more than a day on the yard alone.''

''With the boys' help?''

Frank nodded.

''What if I helped?'' Suddenly Rebecca was aware of three sets of eyes staring at her. ''Just a suggestion.''

To guard against being caught staring at the young minister, Rebecca turned her attention to the soup and corn bread before her, listening only halfheartedly to the conversation between Frank and her father about the cost of repairs to the garage. She was aware Frank was asking much less than she'd expected for the labor and materials that would be needed. He was obviously too idealistic to be a good businessman.

"So, what did you come up with about the boys?" Frank asked Rebecca, startling her out of her reverie.

"I've been more concerned with Mrs. Gruber's problem today," Rebecca said apologetically. "What do *you* think about the boys?" Turning the tables was always a good legal ploy, she reminded herself.

"Briefly, I think it's a matter of the boys having only themselves as company for too much of their lives, the changes of location and . . . well, their mother's death, and their father's remarriage. It's just too much change in their lives for them to cope with," Frank said.

"When their father retired, the boys may have assumed they would have much more of his time to do things that he'd probably been promising them—and that doesn't seem to have materialized. What they did might have been a misdemeanor, but mainly it was a signal to their father that they wanted more of his attention. He probably didn't get the message."

Big Ted nodded his head slowly. "I think you may be on to something," he said. "Everything else is just posturing?"

"I really think so," Frank said. "If their rough language bothers us, they see our reaction and are just pulling our chain, to use a phrase they use. If they went to schools filled with kids like themselves that serve the military bases, either here or abroad, they've learned a very tough way of dealing with the entrenched students they've encountered in new situations."

"I'd been thinking about the same things," Rebecca said, turning down with a gesture the second helping of soup that Margaret was trying to pour into her bowl.

"Look at their tough-guy act this way," Frank said. "They were caught doing something that could have gotten them into real trouble. So what they had to tell the judge is that they can handle whatever punishment he wants to hand out. They're probably marshmallows inside."

"I'm not so sure." Big Ted pushed his chair back and stood up. "We'll just have to wait and see."

"Have you tried to take the paint off the statue of General Blakesley yet?" Rebecca asked Frank, studying his dark eyes, eyes that never seemed far away from smiling.

He laughed, the sound coming warm and genuine to fill the room. "We've tried, but we have a problem. The surface of the statue was already corroded, as bronze gets, and we're trying to find something that will take the paint off without destroying the texture of the work. It will probably have to be something chemical, which will mean that the boys and I won't be able to do it ourselves."

"Why not?" Rebecca asked.

"I'm a carpenter, not a chemist," Frank said. "It's a matter of safety."

"But unless the boys have to repair the damage they've done, they've won," Rebecca protested.

Frank looked across the table at Rebecca for a long moment. "I'd say something about that statue, but you're a native of these parts, and I'm not."

"That the purple paint might be an improvement?" Rebecca suggested cautiously, looking toward where her father had been sitting. She'd been listening so intently that she hadn't realized that her father and mother had left the kitchen. "I suppose you've had to spend a lot of the time you've been working with the boys just teaching them how to do things. I imagine officers' kids don't have to mow lawns."

Frank laughed. "Very true." He stood up and stretched. "I do have to be going now. I knew when I thought of having an evening to myself something would happen."

"I'm sorry we took you away from your own time," Rebecca said apologetically, getting to her feet.

He looked down at her for a long moment, then smiled. "Believe me, Miss Rebecca, it wasn't without its rewards."

She was still wondering if his words had meant what she thought they had when she watched the taillights of his truck leave the driveway.

Had Frank Andrews been flirting with her?

Chapter Four

Rebecca wasn't ready to wake up the next morning. For one thing, thanks to the exertion of clearing away some of the storm damage the night before, she had aches where she hadn't even known she had muscles. Below her window, in the backyard, Frank's truck was idling noisily. Then the motor died with a cough and a sputter.

Her father called out to Frank in the fog-dampened morning, his voice muffled by the veil of oak leaves between him and Rebecca's open window.

Knowing that there was nothing ahead but work this morning, Rebecca dragged herself from her bed and ignored the aches and pains, putting on a pair of comfortably threadbare jeans and an oversize shirt. She yawned mightily as she descended the back stairway and entered the kitchen.

"Good, you're up," her mother said cheerfully, pouring orange juice into glasses on the counter.

"Matter of opinion," Rebecca said, sinking into a chair, forgetting her resolution to be more cheerful in the morning.

"I thought we'd go through the things in the garage attic to see what we can throw away," Margaret said brightly, more alert and ebullient than Rebecca could tolerate. From long experience, however, she knew not to grumble. When she was in this mood she generally ate what was placed in front of her and kept her opinions to herself.

"The electrician will come by at nine, and the insurance adjuster will be here as soon as he can," Big Ted said as he came into the kitchen. "Have you had your breakfast, Frank?"

"Yes, thank you," Frank said.

Rebecca looked up into his eyes, not ready to absorb the electricity with which his eyes attached to hers. She was amazed at how energetic he looked, despite the hour.

"Oh, Frank, you can at least have a cup of coffee," Margaret said, reaching for a mug.

"Well, maybe," Frank said. "I want to start collecting the litter around the yard and take it to the dump. I'll have the boys empty the truck when they get here. I noticed a couple limbs down in neighbors' yards, so I'll send them around to collect those, too."

"The neighbors will appreciate that," Big Ted said.

"Oh!" Margaret exclaimed, handing the mug of coffee to Frank. "I'll have to make something for you and the boys. A big pitcher of lemonade? Yes, I think so. And sandwiches for lunch—"

"Mrs. Hobbs, it's not necessary—" Frank protested.

"Yes, it is. It will save you . . ." Whatever she was saying was lost in the roar of the refrigerator motor as she opened the freezer compartment.

Rebecca took a deep breath and set her jaw. This was going to be a long day, and if she was able to keep up with her mother she would be lucky.

" . . . because I have a round of golf scheduled for eleven this morning," Margaret continued. "But we ought to be finished with whatever we have to do by then, shouldn't we, Rebecca?"

Rebecca rubbed her eyes. "I guess so."

She applied herself to filling the bowl at her place with Raisin Bran and drowning it in milk. How her father had ever changed from bacon and eggs to grapefruit and bran cereal she would never fathom. To be honest, she really wanted a cherry Danish, covered with enough gooey frosting to endanger any legal paper that dared to get too close to her long fingernails for the rest of the morning. Willpower and mornings just didn't mix.

Outside, metal scraped against the wooden posts of the porch and heavy footsteps thumped on the risers and boomed across the porch floor to the door to the central hall.

"In here, boys!" Margaret called.

The Blakesley twins, identical as two morning glories on the same vine to the casual observer, strolled into the kitchen, a blur of blond hair, blue eyes, white T-shirts and blue jeans. They greeted everyone politely, with a particularly distinct "Good morning, Your Honor" to Big Ted and a subdued "How d'ya do, Miss Rebecca" in her direction when she was introduced.

Rebecca couldn't believe they were any kind of trouble at all. Aside from the fact that they were in her mother's kitchen at a particularly unattractive time in the morning, they were eminently tolerable.

They turned down Margaret's offer of food and went back outside with directions to unload the ladders and lawn tools from the truck and begin loading it with the limbs sheared from the fallen tree the night before, especially the ones in front of the garage door.

They'd just left the kitchen when the insurance adjuster arrived to begin his calculations. Margaret was in her glory, pouring coffee and making herself inconspicuously indispensable. Rebecca chased the last raisin around the bottom of her bowl and decided that there was no way she was going to be able to put off the inevitable any longer. In the interests of feeling justified in sunning herself later, she would pitch in and help this morning, while the air was cool and still.

She picked up small branches in the yard, keeping a keen ear on the negotiations being carried on by Big Ted, the insurance adjuster and Frank Andrews—temporarily wearing the hat of a handyman.

One foot braced on the rear bumper of his truck, Frank was sketching on a drafting pad and figuring as quickly as he could.

"We can't possibly replace that old brickwork, because we can't come near to the bricks made back when the garage was built," Big Ted was saying.

"Maybe we can just close it with shingles." Frank said something about a bearing wall and support for rafters and a lot of other things that Rebecca didn't understand, but he sounded very knowledgeable, and she felt a growing respect for him—until he read off the figure to the insurance adjuster.

Rebecca stopped in the middle of picking up a heavy limb and stared at him. She would have asked for more money for this job. After all, he'd spent two hours the night before helping to secure the gaping hole in the roof and side of the garage, and he'd cleared the way to get the station wagon out of the garage if it was needed. Her training in business told her he certainly deserved more.

The Blakesley twins, whose individual names Rebecca had yet to attach securely to them, didn't seem to have mastered the art of being unobtrusive or quiet as they piled limbs into the back of the truck or filled the wheelbarrow with leaves. Frank had had to remind them several times to be quiet while he'd done his figuring.

Margaret, finished with her breakfast chores, came out to the yard dressed in slacks and a blouse, ready to tackle the chore of sorting out the mess, motioning for Rebecca to follow her.

Rebecca, whose back had protested every stretch and lift of the past quarter hour, found climbing the steps to the attic a new experience in pain.

"I suppose we'll have to come up with a new yard display for Christmas this year," Margaret said with a sigh, surveying a plywood table that had been flattened.

"Not that this one hasn't given years of service," Rebecca muttered.

Margaret brightened. "It will give your father something to do when the baseball season is over. I've always wanted him to build an animated display, but he says that's too complicated. I contend he's just too lazy to work it all out. And he says if he'd wanted to be a mechanical engineer he'd have gone to Georgia Tech, not Duke."

Rebecca didn't have to be reminded of the discussion that generally took up a Saturday afternoon early in November every year. Margaret would broach creative ideas, Big Ted would plead technical ignorance, and the same stable scene would be erected in the yard two weeks before Christmas. This year, Margaret's joyful attitude seemed to say, would be different.

"Can we be any help?" one of the boys called up from the yard below.

"Not just yet," Margaret called back, then turned to Rebecca. "These things are a total loss, don't you think?"

Rebecca nodded and began sorting through the pile for anything salvageable, knowing in her heart that nothing could be saved of the display that had fascinated her as a child.

Frank's voice drifted up to her from below. "Come on, boys. I want you to follow along on your bikes over to the dump, then come back here while I get a building permit at the courthouse and line up the supplies we need."

"Yes, sir," the boys responded automatically.

One boy wiped a hand on his shirttail, leaving a greenish-brown smudge. They both mounted their expensive-looking ten-speed bikes and followed the truck out to the street.

"They seem like good little workers, don't they?" Margaret said. "I can't see how they can be such problems."

Rebecca nodded, feeling each adjustment in her muscles as she moved. "They seem normal for their age and background."

Margaret made a disgusted face at the litter in the attic. "I think it will be easier to just remove all this while the wall is open. But I hate to just pitch everything down to the driveway."

"It can wait until the boys come back to help us," Rebecca said, and her mother nodded in agreement.

"I can't work on this much longer," Margaret said. "I have some errands to run before I go to play golf."

"I need to go over to the courthouse, too, to check on the status of Mrs. Gruber's house."

"Oh, yes!" Margaret said, as though she'd totally forgotten about Rebecca's project for the elderly woman. "Well, now would be a good time to take care of that."

"I can't go over looking like this," she said with a laugh, looking down at her jeans. "No one would take me seriously."

There was a particular scent in the courthouse, especially in the tax collector's office on the first floor, that was oddly comforting to Rebecca. It had something to do with reams of paper, furniture polish and coffee, and it reminded Rebecca of the orderliness that she'd always admired about the practice of law.

There was the hum and clatter of office machinery that had not been updated unnecessarily. The county neither needed nor could it afford a great expenditure on sophisticated computers. Rebecca took some comfort in that.

An older woman dressed in a gray blouse with a soft, demure bow at the collar came to the counter and offered to help Rebecca. When Rebecca told her what she wanted, the frail woman searched another area of the office, then carried a bulky ledger over to the counter, found the proper page and turned it so that Rebecca could read the entries concerning Mrs. Gruber's property.

"Is this all that Mrs. Gruber owes on that property?" Rebecca asked, tracing the figure with a fingernail that was a little the worse for wear after this morning. "For this ERM can take over that piece of property to build a shopping plaza?"

The clerk, who was holding on to the ledger on the counter as though Rebecca were about to make off with it, nodded her gray head silently, and Rebecca looked away for just a moment to check the figure she'd written on the back of an envelope.

"All anyone needs to take title to one of these properties is to pay off the taxes," the woman said, pointing to the page.

The amount that was due was about the same as the refund she expected from canceling her trip to London. She tried to weigh the alternatives, but they all involved time-consuming maneuvers and hearings and were rife with opportunities for legal chicanery. She really didn't have time for that if at any minute a representative of ERM could write out a check and claim the property.

Rebecca had visions of a bulldozer lumbering across Mrs. Gruber's lawn and biting into the veranda while lawyers served papers and committees argued.

"Will you take a personal check?" Rebecca asked impulsively, mentally reviewing the balance in her checking account.

"Well, we'd prefer a cashier's check, but considering you're Judge Hobbs's daughter—"

"I don't expect any favors," Rebecca said. "But if I can pay off her taxes so easily I'd be afraid that if I left this office to go over to the bank for a cashier's check someone from ERM Properties would slip in here and snap this property up before I got back."

The clerk, who'd listened sympathetically, motioned for the tax collector himself to decide on the issue.

"Well, since you *are* Judge Hobbs's daughter," he said, "and since it's Mrs. Gruber's property, I guess it would be all right." He went away grumbling about the county being better off without big-city people coming in and taking over.

Rebecca gladly made out the check.

"We'll have your title to the property ready by close of business this afternoon," the clerk said. "I'll send the papers up to your father's office."

"No! The property is to stay in Mrs. Gruber's name," Rebecca protested.

"I'm sorry," the tax collector, who'd overheard her protest, said firmly. "I have to comply with the law. If you want to return the property to Mrs. Gruber later, you can do that at your leisure. But the law says we have to deed the land to you.''

Rebecca took a deep breath. It was just another detail she would have to take care of. Rebecca merely smiled back at them and left. She was going to drop by Mrs. Gruber's and give her the receipt for the payment on her taxes, but she saw the Blakesley boys sauntering along the sidewalk, pushing their bikes and drinking from cans of soda pop, so she decided that she ought to go back home and get back into her working clothes, if only to keep an eye on them.

Frank stared out the window of the planning and zoning office in the courthouse, waiting for a clerk to get back to him. Suddenly he saw something out the window that made the pencil in his hand stop its rhythmic tattoo on the clipboard on the counter in front of him.

The newly familiar figure of Rebecca Hobbs strolled down the courthouse steps, slim and confident, moving as though she hadn't a care in the world. Her short brown hair gleamed in the morning sunlight as she looked one way and then another, giving him a moment to contemplate the way it feathered against the nape of her neck, far above the scooped back of her light summer blouse. She'd gotten some sun recently; her skin was slightly pink, but it would probably tan soon enough. A breeze ruffled her skirt to define her slender legs and softly rounded hips.

Strange what even this glimpse of Rebecca did to him. He was too old for a schoolboy crush, but all the symptoms were there—sleeplessness, lack of concentration, this exhilaration when he caught the slightest glimpse of her.

For years he hadn't allowed himself to have lustful thoughts like those he'd entertained since Monday evening. After all, he'd been in college, then seminary, and then a foreign land for a while. Another older, wiser minister had taken him aside and warned him not to get emotionally involved with a woman under those circumstances, considering that his time in each place was limited. He thought he should tell himself that same thing now as he watched Rebecca cross the square to where her flashy little car was parked.

And for him a relationship had to be all or nothing. Marriage was the only option for a man of the cloth, a long and faithful marriage. So the woman had to be special. It occurred to him that every new facet of Rebecca's personality that was revealed to him placed another checkmark on his list of wife-material requirements, and the marks all seemed to be lining up dangerously in the Favorable column. Dangerous, because at the moment he had precious little to offer, and he felt she might find someone more worth her while around the next corner. To let his feelings keep escalating, as they seemed to do hourly, he risked emotional involvement that would cost him dearly if she didn't return his attentions. It was best to ignore the infatuation and stick to business, he tried to tell himself.

But two nearly sleepless nights told him that the caution came too late. He was aching for a time when they could sit and talk, not about anything in particular, but about what they thought, what they had in common. On occasion, his thoughts had run on to activities more intimate than conversation, but with great self-control he kept them in line now.

Then he saw the boys pushing their bikes along the sidewalk in the direction of the Hobbs house and remembered that he had a job to do.

"Have you finished those papers yet, sir?" a clerk asked him.

Frank smiled and pushed the clipboard across the counter. "I think I've filled in everything I can," he said. Then he shook his head. Red tape and pretty women.

Nothing really changed, no matter where you went.

"Hey, watch what you're doin', stupid."

"I can't help it if you're a wimp!"

"Keep it down, both of you!" Rebecca yelled at the boys, who were arguing like magpies as they cleared the trash from the attic of the garage. "All you do is argue, and it's getting on my nerves!"

The look they gave her informed Rebecca that her opinion held no weight with them. Sullenly they returned to the task, speaking to each other just enough to signal for caution. They spoke in a sort of shorthand; they clearly knew each other well enough that nothing more was needed.

Frank showed up with a grim look on his face. "All we can do today is clear away the debris," he said, waving a slip of paper. "An inspector has to look at the building, then approve my plans."

"Can't you get them to hurry things along?" Rebecca asked. "We don't pull rank very often, but I'm sure if they knew it was for my father—"

"This is the best I could do, even *with* your father's name," Frank said. "Otherwise we'd be waiting until next week."

Margaret heard him as she came out of the house, dressed to play her round of golf at the Kerry Knolls Country Club. "Well, do the best you can," she told him. "Why don't you all go into the kitchen and have some lemonade and cookies?"

She proceeded into the garage and opened the back of her station wagon to put her golf clubs inside, but before she could reach for them one of the boys scrambled to hoist the heavy bag for her. "Why, thank you, Timmy," she said, beaming at him.

The other boy, not to be outdone, opened the door of the car for her. *What has she got that I don't have?* Rebecca asked herself, smiling and waving to her mother as she backed the car into the newly cleared turn around and from there drove out onto the street.

"Lemonade and cookies, guys!" she called to the boys.

"Got anything stronger?" one of them asked.

"Take what you're offered and be satisfied," Frank said, following them into the kitchen.

Margaret had set the pitcher of lemonade and the plate of cookies on the kitchen table. The boys washed their hands at the sink and dried them on the thighs of their jeans.

They seemed to count the cookies before deciding how many to take. Then they shouldered their way out to the porch with the cookies in one hand and the glasses of lemonade Rebecca had poured in the other.

"I don't understand them," Rebecca told Frank softly, not wanting them to overhear. "They treat Mama as though she were a queen, and they're barely civil to me. Of course, I *did* speak to them rather sharply. Maybe I shouldn't have."

Frank shrugged, looking around for a towel to dry his hands on. "When I have them figured out, I'll tell you," he said, his dark eyes smiling.

Rebecca placed a glass of lemonade on the table for him and proceeded to pour one for herself. Slowly she eased herself into a chair and picked up one of the plump oatmeal cookies. "What sort of formula do you use to figure out what you charge for a job like this?" she asked.

"Well, ten dollars an hour plus the cost of materials," Frank told her.

"And what do you pay the boys?"

"Minimum wage, of course."

"You're paying two thirteen-year-olds minimum wage?"

"Should I pay them more?"

"No! Good gracious! That's too much!" Rebecca said, nearly choking on her cookie. "Look, they're working for you as punishment! You're paying them so much they're making out like bandits!"

"But what else am I supposed to do?"

"Good question," Rebecca said thoughtfully. "But think of it this way. What's a kid going to do with that much money, in a town like Blakesley Hills, of all places?"

"I take out taxes and social security," Frank said defensively.

"Have you looked at the child-labor laws?" Rebecca asked.

"I don't make them work more than six or seven hours a day," Frank said. "Besides, it's summer."

"But aren't you giving them around a hundred dollars a week?"

"Closer to eighty."

"I'd say you should be putting all but ten in the bank for them, preferably in trust, so they can't touch it," Rebecca suggested. She looked at him and suddenly felt a little defensive, afraid he would take offense at her for offering advice. "But what disturbs me more is that if you're charging only ten dollars an hour for labor and paying them minimum, you're actually making less than minimum yourself, because you also have the overhead to worry about."

"I don't need a lot," Frank told her. "All I have is the truck. Your aunt is letting me use your uncle's old tools. So long as I can make ends meet I'll be happy."

"I know very well I'm probably way out of line here," Rebecca said, leaning forward on her elbows and looking at him earnestly. "Your training is in academic and theoretical fields, but I know something about business because of my training in law, and I think you're charging too little and paying the boys too much.''

''I can't just go to the boys and tell them I'm not going to pay them as much as I promised,'' Frank told her, more distressed at the idea she presented than at her effrontery in expressing it. ''Going back on my word is against my principles.''

''If you set up a trust for their education with the remainder of the money, they would still be getting the money in the long run, when they are more mature and less apt to run amok.''

Frank gave her a long look that she couldn't readily interpret. Then he shifted in his chair.

''As for charging more,'' Frank said after a thoughtful moment, ''I'm doing work for members of the congregation—''

''That's no reason to let them take advantage of you,'' Rebecca argued. ''Daddy, for one, can afford to pay you decently. Look at it this way. There's nothing particularly ethical about undercutting the other people who do similar work and have more than themselves to look out for.''

''I never thought of it that way,'' Frank said slowly.

Obviously Frank needed some time to think about the wages he was paying the boys, because when they returned to their work he didn't say anything about it.

The building inspector came just as they were about to break for lunch, and Rebecca was thankful for a chance to cool off in the kitchen and make herself a sandwich. The boys slipped away on their bikes, probably to go home for lunch, and when she no longer heard any voices in the yard she looked out and found that both Frank and the inspector had left.

''Perfect!'' Rebecca exclaimed, only slightly disappointed that she wouldn't have a quiet lunch with Frank all to herself. What a great time to grab a quick sandwich, soak in a cool tub and then check in on Mrs. Gruber.

Rebecca had learned from her visit to Agnes Gruber the day before that it was best to go to the side door of the old house. There was an air-conditioning unit in the window there, and Agnes spent her time sitting in a lounger, watching television.

Rebecca was a little hesitant at first. She thought it might be best for her to explain who she was again, in case Mrs. Gruber had forgotten.

But the elderly woman smiled and unlatched the screen door to let her in. "Of course I remember who you are," she assured her. "Look, I found the papers I couldn't get to yesterday. I'm afraid, though, that I've waited too long— Oh, would you like tea, dear?"

"No, thank you," Rebecca told her. "I just had lunch." Tea the day before had been a scalding hot cup of something that had tasted a little strange, and Rebecca had had to console herself with the thought that it didn't seem strong enough to do any real damage.

She took the papers Agnes handed her and held them toward the window to read them. "Well, it's all moot now," she said, handing them back to Mrs. Gruber. "I've taken care of one thing."

In order to encourage Mrs. Gruber to stop flitting around and sit down on her lounger, Rebecca sat tentatively on a straight-backed chair and looked at her earnestly.

"I paid the taxes on your house, Mrs. Gruber," she stated simply.

"Oh, my!" Agnes said. "Now you own it—"

"Well, that's true," Rebecca said, concerned by the confusion and fear that showed in the woman's face.

"Where will I go? My niece has been after me to move in with her, but—"

"Now, now, Mrs. Gruber," Rebecca said. "I have no intention of putting you out of your house. You can stay here just as long as you want. I, ah . . . just have to work a few things out."

"I can't pay rent," Agnes complained. "I can't. It's all I can do to pay the electricity and insurance and feed myself."

"I'm not asking for rent," Rebecca said, trying to reassure her. "I don't want anything from you. I just want you to live here and be comfortable. I don't want you to worry about anything."

She didn't leave until she was certain that Mrs. Gruber understood that she wouldn't have to leave her home. It was a struggle.

On the way home, Rebecca was struck by the many new problems she'd created for herself. She owned a house now, and she had no idea what to do with it.

Chapter Five

Rebecca returned home to a scene of confusion. A building supplies truck had arrived with the materials needed to patch the garage, and the boys were helping two burly men unload lumber and shingles while Frank supervised. His brow was creased with concern.

"What's wrong?" Rebecca asked him as he wiped the sheen of perspiration from his tanned face on the sleeves of his black T-shirt.

"Well, for a start, the county inspector thinks we ought to replace more of the rafters than I had planned on," he told her. He smiled down at her with grudging respect. "I guess you were right after all about what this job should cost. I called the insurance adjuster, and he said he thought my estimate was low, too."

Rebecca shook her head. "It gives me no joy to be right about this," she told him. "What did Daddy say about it?"

Frank shrugged his powerful shoulders and braced his hands on the hips of his low-slung jeans. "I haven't been able to talk it over with him yet," he told her. "I can't do much except clear away the damage until we discuss it."

The driver who'd delivered the building supplies handed Frank a clipboard holding the invoice for the shipment. Frank checked it over before signing his name. He sent one of the boys to count the pieces of lumber and the other to count the clapboard shingles. Rebecca watched in amusement at the efficient way the boys counted and reported back smartly so that there was no chance of being misunderstood.

When the driver returned to his truck, Rebecca started back to the house. "Lemonade for everybody!" she proclaimed.

They sat on the back porch with their tall glasses, enjoying what shade and breeze there was for a few minutes.

"You know what I did today?" Rebecca asked, shaking her head as new aspects of the magnitude of her action hit her. "I bought Mrs. Gruber's house for the taxes due on it."

"You're kidding!" Frank exclaimed.

"I wish I were," Rebecca said.

"That weird old place?" one of the twins asked.

"If it were painted a lighter color," Rebecca said, "it wouldn't look weird. It's just always been painted brown."

"You going to live there?" the other boy asked her.

"No," Rebecca answered quickly. "Mrs. Gruber is going to live there as long as she wants to."

"So it's not going to be a shopping plaza?" he asked.

"No. Not if I can help it."

"No bank, supermarket, drugstore, pizza place and video arcade?"

"No."

"Shucks."

"There are already places like that in town," Rebecca pointed out.

The boys groaned, as though they were giving up on her ever understanding their hopes of civilization as they knew it coming to Blakesley Hills.

"Aw, c'mon, fellas," Frank said. "The town isn't so bad."

"Whatta *you* know?" the twin with the smudged T-shirt asked. "Straight out of a jungle where the nearest ice-cream cone was three hundred miles away."

Frank's tanned face split into a broad grin. "It wasn't quite like that."

"Weren't you glad to get back, though?" the more assertive twin asked.

"Yes," Frank admitted. "Yes, I was."

"What did you appreciate most when you got back?" the other one asked.

Frank thought for a long moment. "The sound of things I could understand without having to translate them. Even after I became fluent in Spanish I was still constantly translating measurements and money. It's a strain, and you don't realize it until you don't have to put up with it anymore."

"What about food? When we were overseas I was always looking for donuts and—pizza and—"

"Boiled peanuts—"

"Yeah! And grits!"

"Grits?" Rebecca said with a laugh. "How could you be lonesome for grits?"

"With bacon crumpled up and some brown sugar," the boy said, rolling his blue eyes heavenward.

"He's weird!" the other twin said, giving his brother a friendly push. "Grits should have a little salt and lots of butter. Not margarine, butter!"

Rebecca laughed. "Grits are best when they're served with someone else's breakfast! What do you think, Frank?"

He laughed and shook his head. "I'm not going to get into this one," he said, but his dark eyes were amused. "Back to work, guys," he said, having finished his lemonade long since.

He gave Rebecca a lingering smile. "Are you taking the rest of the day off?" he asked.

"Do you mean I'm being invited to help this afternoon?" Rebecca asked, aware that she was flirting with this man. It was easier to think of him as a carpenter than as a minister, and for a moment she lost sight of his calling altogether.

"Well, if you can't keep up with us you're welcome to be a sidewalk superintendent," Frank said with a laugh, and left the porch with long strides that took him across the yard to the garage.

Scowling momentarily, the boys left their glasses on the table, quietly thanked Rebecca for the lemonade and hurried after Frank.

Rebecca picked up the empty glasses and took them inside.

She'd fully intended to get some sun this afternoon, but it seemed tactless to lie out in the sun while the fellows worked on the garage. Yes, that would be all wrong.

Rebecca slipped into her shorts and a fresh T-shirt and returned to the backyard, just in time to hear a great hoot of laughter coming from the second floor of the garage.

"C'mon guys, we have a lot to get done yet today," Frank said sharply to the boys as they rooted through a box that had come open as they'd tried to move it.

"Wow!"

"Neat stuff!"

Tim put something on his face while Jim pulled a wig over his blond hair. Frank sighed. When the boys were distracted, it was difficult to get their attention back on the business at hand.

Resigning himself to a short delay, Frank turned to catch the breeze that came into the loft from the opening. His breath caught as he saw Rebecca start down the steps of the back porch, her long legs bare from the tops of her sneakers to the cuffs of her shorts. *Why does she do this to me?* he asked himself. Then he realized that it wasn't her fault he got tongue-tied when he saw her. She was just being herself. Her effervescent, elegant, witty self.

Running up the stairs, Rebecca was greeted by one twin wearing a pair of fake glasses and big nose and the other wearing a rainbow-colored wig.

"Oh, great! You found my brother Don's box of practical jokes!" she said, grinning back at the boys.

"Come on, guys," Frank growled impatiently as he bent to hoist a box that was in the way of something he wanted to do. "Settle down. We have work to do. Becca, we have to move more of the boxes so I can bring some lumber up here."

"Sure," Rebecca said, wiping her hands on her shirt and picking her way across the littered floor to help with the chore. Frank's shortening of her proper name to what her family often called her felt so natural she didn't even question it. "My brother Don is a monster with practical jokes, guys. You'd be doing Mama and me a favor if you'd help yourself to whatever you want out of that box."

"Don't give them any ideas," Frank cautioned, hoisting a heavy box onto his powerful shoulders.

Rebecca had expected him to go a different way around some boxes, and they bumped into each other. "Pardon," she said under her breath, embarrassed by her uncharacteristic clumsiness.

Frank paused, his back to the boys, and winked. "The pleasure was all mine," he murmured softly.

Surprised, Rebecca looked up at him and smiled, but he was already moving across the room, his jeans-clad hips swiveling as he avoided one obstacle after another.

The boys, having removed their disguises and tossed them back in the box, were trying to find something else of interest. She saw them nod to each other and stuff something into their pockets. They looked at her questioningly, and for some reason she winked back. She thought she knew just about everything that was in that box, and if she could stay at a reasonable distance she might avoid getting a plastic spider dropped down her back.

Frank, on the other hand, had no inkling of what was to come. When the lethal-looking tarantula landed on his shoulder, he jumped two feet and said something he certainly hadn't learned at the seminary. Rebecca was convulsed more by the innocent looks on the twins' faces than by Frank's reaction.

When Frank looked accusingly at her, Rebecca was laughing too hard to defend herself.

"I don't think these things are funny," Frank roared.

"Yes, sir," the boys chorused sharply.

Rebecca was disappointed in his reaction. She loved the way he laughed, and she didn't mind harmless jokes—so long as they were played on someone else.

As Rebecca helped shift Hobbs family flotsam and jetsam around in the next few minutes, she was more than slightly aware that she was the center of Frank's attention and that the boys were watching them closely.

When Frank declared that enough space had been cleared to bring in the lumber he needed, he and the boys trooped downstairs. The second floor of the carriage house was oppressively hot and dusty, but Rebecca couldn't think of a good reason to leave.

Below the ragged opening in the side of the garage, Frank and the boys squabbled about how much lumber the boys could safely carry up to the second floor. Their estimates were far greater than his. They were showing off to repair any damage they had done in playing their prank on him.

They all struggled back up the steps and stacked the lumber in the cleared space. Rebecca leaned against a pile of boxes and watched them head downstairs for a second load.

While she caught her breath, she listened to the boys. They were being too quiet, she thought. It was the calm before a storm; she could sense it.

When Frank sent them back down for the last of the lumber he wanted moved, she followed him to where he was studying his plans.

"Tactical error, Frank," she said in a cautious voice. "They're up to something, and you shouldn't have let them out of your sight."

"They're all right," he said, unconcerned, putting the plans down. In fact, he'd felt a change in their feelings toward Rebecca in the last few minutes. She'd won them over by laughing at their antics and letting them have the junk in the box they'd found. He felt a twinge of something unworthy and tried to rise above it. "Of course, if you don't want to be alone—"

His dark eyes were flashing at her and his smile was mischievous. Rebecca raised her chin a few degrees, not expecting such a blatantly flirtatious attitude from him. "Why, I wouldn't think a couple young'ns like them would cramp your style," she drawled theatrically.

"The secret is to wear them out," Frank said.

"What then?" Rebecca asked.

Frank looked at her for a long moment, then laughed. "I don't know. I'm usually worn out by then, too!"

Rebecca and Frank were laughing when the boys returned to the attic, carefully adding the last pieces to the pile of lumber. Then both boys came close to Frank and studied the plans in his hands.

"Now what do you need?" the twin with the smudged shirt asked. Rebecca reasoned in a flash that he must be Tim, the one who always took the lead. He also had a slightly deeper cleft in his chin. Now she could tell them apart!

"I'll need the big tool—"

Suddenly a spring-coiled snake exploded from the plans in front of Frank. In reaction, Rebecca fell backward onto a dusty old beanbag chair, which split at the seam that had been taped closed long ago. The little plastic beans inside flew everywhere, raining on the bare plank floor like a spattering of buckshot.

The boys doubled over in laughter; their joke had caused more havoc than they could possibly have anticipated.

Frank bellowed something he immediately regretted. "You two can leave right now," he shouted. "You're nothing but trouble."

Embarrassed and shocked by Frank's outburst, Rebecca struggled to her feet, dusting the seat of her shorts and trying to catch her breath. "Frank . . . really . . ."

"You can't send us home!" Tim protested.

"There's too much work to do."

"And it takes two people."

"At least!"

The twins turned toward Rebecca, as though they didn't consider her capable of toting and hauling.

"Then sweep up this mess!" Frank ordered. "We can't be slipping and falling on those—those things."

"There's a utility vacuum down in the workshop," Rebecca told the boys calmly, turning away from Frank. "It'll make short work of this."

"Right!" the boys chorused, hurrying down the stairs.

Frank let out a long breath, as though he were counting. "Miss Rebecca, I apologize for my temper. It's my biggest failing. And these boys test it continuously."

"I'll just—I'm in the way," Rebecca said. "I'll go do something else."

The look he gave her, tortured regret, made her pause. She stepped aside to let the boys maneuver the bulky vacuum into the cleared space and backed away to the stairs. She pointed out the electrical outlet to them, then hurried down the steps and across the yard.

The twins were laughing above the roar of the vacuum, and Frank watched her return to the house. He'd made a mess of things, of course. Maybe it was because he was so out of practice. He'd been too controlled, too single-minded, to care so much about a woman for so long, he didn't know how to handle the situation. It was beneath him to feel jealous of the attention Rebecca gave the twins or the way they responded to her. It was selfish of him to want all her smiles directed at him.

He wondered if he was in love. Whatever he was feeling, it was uncomfortable, untimely and unwise. But, God, it felt good!

"How's it going?" Big Ted called to Frank as he got out of his car.

Frank turned from measuring the plank he was about to saw. "We've got problems," he stated flatly. "This job is going to take a little longer than I expected."

"That's no big deal," Big Ted said, waving to the boys, who were clambering down from the ladders leaning against the garage.

"The county inspector wants us to replace more rafters," Frank told him. "I already called the insurance company about it. I—I guess I underestimated."

"I thought you were cutting it a little close, Frank. And I don't mind going to the added expense."

"I wanted to get this hole closed by the time we finished today, but we're all pretty tired, huh, boys? I think we'd better put the tarpaulin back up and call it a day."

"Yeah!" Tim agreed. "C'mon, we'll take care of it." Jim followed him up the ladder.

Frank decided to let them figure out how to rig the tarp themselves; after all, they'd helped him take it down that morning.

"Miss Rebecca gave me a lesson in cost-estimating this morning," Frank said, bracing his foot on the pile of lumber.

Big Ted laughed. "That's part of her business, you know? Knowing how much it's going to cost to do things so that the contracts she writes are fair to the company she works for."

Frank idly straightened up the area where he'd been working. "She's a smart woman," he said, wondering if Big Ted would read anything into the remark, wondering if he could keep certain feelings out of his voice.

"Yes, she is that," Big Ted said proudly. "Smart and spirited. A lot like her mother."

Big Ted wandered off toward the house while Frank and the boys secured their project for the night. The boys didn't have to be told twice that they were free to go home. They hopped on their bikes and were off, talking about the things they were going to do with their evening.

Frank stood staring at the garage for a long moment, thinking not about the job he had to do the next day but about the young woman who lived in the house behind him.

Smart and spirited, her father had called her.

She was more than that. Working here, yearning to get a glimpse of her, to sit and talk to her, was getting to be a distraction. A pleasant distraction, but a distraction nonetheless.

Rebecca was sitting in the kitchen, snapping green beans for dinner, when her father entered from the back porch.

"I've got something for you here," Big Ted said, taking a thick envelope from his jacket pocket.

"Hmmm," Rebecca said. "I was just thinking about that. I think I made a mistake."

"Now what did you do?" Big Ted asked, giving her a look she remembered from her childhood. It had usually been well deserved back then, when she tended to act first and think afterward. Her training in law should have eliminated that trait from her character, but there was something about being home again that had led her to revert to her old, impetuous ways.

"I paid Mrs. Gruber's taxes," Rebecca said, bracing herself for her father's reaction.

"You did?" he asked, freezing as he turned to open the refrigerator door in search of something cold to drink.

"Um. She really didn't owe a lot. It's just that one year she forgot to pay, then the next year she'd been sick and had some big medical bills. By the third year, the bill was just too much to handle on her tight budget."

Big Ted stared at her for a long moment. "What are you going to do with a place like that?"

"Nothing!" Rebecca said, snapping the last bean and lifting the colander out of her lap to place it on the counter by the sink. "I was planning to sign the house over to her, but now I'm having second thoughts. I was just sitting here thinking about it, and I realized that if I signed the house back over to her the same thing would probably happen all over again. And I think she deserves a break. She shouldn't have to pay taxes anymore."

"So?" Big Ted asked.

"I've already told her she can live there as long as she likes," Rebecca said. "She doesn't have anywhere else to go except to move in with a niece who's almost as old as she is. I don't want to charge her rent. But now I'm stuck with the taxes every year, and I just remembered I'm out of work myself."

"Purely a temporary matter, I'm sure," Ted said, glossing over that fact confidently.

Rebecca drained the last of her iced tea, then stood up and put the glass in the dishwasher. "Well, it's a consideration. Suddenly I'm a landowner, and I don't know what to do about it."

Ted laughed. "I have a feeling we've been here once or twice before."

Rebecca grinned at him, a bit sheepishly. "I was just thinking about that, too."

"Well, if you ask me, I think you did the right thing at the moment, if your objective was to keep Mrs. Gruber in her home. Your problems are just beginning, though." Ted smiled and started toward the stairs.

"You really bought Mrs. Gruber's house?" Margaret asked, coming into the kitchen. The acoustics in the kitchen were such that secrets were impossible to keep. "Wait until I tell Thelma!"

"Mom! Don't tell everybody—"

"But it will be a matter of public record anyway," Margaret said. "And Thelma was really worried about it. She'll be so pleased the development company isn't getting that property."

"But I don't know what I'm going to do with it just yet."

Margaret looked across the room at her, just as she reached for the telephone. "So you're worried about paying the taxes. Darling, things can always be worked out. Mothers always have little bits of money stashed away for emergencies."

"Mom, I couldn't—"

"It's for Mrs. Gruber, dear." Margaret started to dial a number.

Rebecca turned away and looked out the window toward the garage.

Frank was standing by his truck, checking over his plans before tossing them back on the seat. He folded himself behind the wheel and slammed the door closed.

The truck coughed and sputtered, then began to tremble as he backed it into the turnaround.

Against her will, Rebecca turned so that she could catch a glimpse of the truck as it passed the dining room window. It was another familiar moment, like when she'd gotten up at a quarter of six so that she could catch a glimpse of Buddy Joe Gibson when he delivered the morning paper. It was the same, and yet so much more. There was something about Frank Andrews that scared the dickens out of her.

She rinsed the green beans under the faucet and set them in the sink to drain.

"Mama, if you don't have anything more for me to do I think I'll go take a shower," she said, and started upstairs without really waiting for an answer.

Frank hadn't realized how late it was when he'd changed to go over to the church and conduct the Bible-study class. Miss Ruth had fretted that he hadn't eaten enough, promising to leave a piece of cake in the refrigerator for him to have when he got home.

His black tunic felt hot around his shoulders as he hurried the two blocks to the church. He would have taken the truck, but it was almost as quick to walk, and it was less aggravation. Generally the walk gave him a few minutes to think over what he was going to say in his lesson, but this evening his thoughts weren't so easily regimented.

It was unsettling to have Rebecca Hobbs intruding on his thoughts, but she was never far from them these days. Even when he was able to concentrate on something he'd look up and she'd be there, in living, breathing flesh. Or else something she had said to him would come crashing into his consciousness. Like when the county inspector was outlining changes that would be needed for the garage. She'd been right! He didn't run his business the way it should be run. His records were barely acceptable, but he'd thought that he would straighten all that out later.

Unfortunately, *later* seemed to be filled with other, more important things.

This evening sometime he would have to sit down with his calculator and refigure his formula. It wasn't fair to put temptation in front of the boys by paying them too much. Nor was it fair to underbid other men who did the same work.

When he entered the church's meeting hall, he was glad there were people there. It forced him to think of something other than Rebecca Hobbs and his handyman business. This was, after all, his primary work, the calling he'd pledged his life to.

He only hoped the homily he'd prepared for this evening was interesting enough to hold the attention of the dozen or so parishioners who would show up. They were a small group, but they were surprisingly well-read in Scripture.

Discussions grew lively, challenging him more than he'd expected. It would probably shock these people to know that he was still growing in his faith, when they looked to him for answers because of his seminary training and his experience. He suspected he had a lot to learn from them as well.

After spending a few minutes chatting with the members of the group, Frank walked to the front of the room, placed his Bible on the podium and read the evening's Scripture to them. This was comfortable, he acknowledged silently, taking a deep breath. This was where he belonged.

"So you see, boys, it will all work out," Frank said after his long explanation of why he couldn't pay them as much as he'd told them he would, that he would give most of their wages to their father to place in their savings accounts and that by the time they were ready to go to college it would all even out.

Tim's blue eyes narrowed as he paused before hammering a nail. "So you're not paying us as much as you said you were going to?"

"Well, in the long run, you'll get the same." Frank said, trying to mollify him.

"But if you paid us what you promised us and put some of it in the bank we'd have even more when we went to college," Tim said. "Besides, do you trust our father to put the money in our accounts?"

"Of course I do!" Frank said, setting a nail in a shingle with a sound tap, then driving it with three quick blows.

"Humph!" Jim said in protest.

"What's that supposed to mean?" Frank asked, reaching into the pocket of his carpenter's apron for another nail.

The boys turned hardened looks on him. Something was going on in their minds that Frank knew nothing about. They didn't talk much about deep, substantive issues, particularly where their family was concerned, so he had few clues as to what they thought.

He went back to what he'd been doing, and in a moment the boys were hammering away again. Frank thought, from the sound of their hammers, that they must be angry. Their faces, when he caught glimpses of them, were grim.

The morning had been partly cloudy, and the occasional break from full sun had been a blessing when they'd worked on the roof and the sunny side of the garage. Now that it was approaching noon and the sun was high, the cloud cover had become thicker and more frequent.

"I think we'd better get this all closed in before we break for lunch, fellows," Frank said. "Then if it rains this afternoon it won't matter."

"Can we take the afternoon off?" Tim asked.

"It looks like we'll have to." Frank looked around to see how much more work had to be done. "We may have to come back to this later."

"Sure," Jim said.

"Hey up there!" Rebecca called from the yard below. "Isn't it about time for lunch?"

"We're trying to finish up here," Frank said. "Looks like rain."

"Then I guess I'll have to go tell Mama you don't want the sandwiches she was going to make for you."

"Tell her thanks but no thanks," Frank said. "We're going to close this all in, then call it quits for the day."

"First the money, now the sandwiches," Tim muttered and Jim made a sound of agreement.

Chapter Six

The boys had already trundled off on their bikes when Rebecca went back out into the yard to take another message to Frank. "Mama wants you to come to dinner tonight," she told him as he put his saw back into his toolbox.

"She's bound and determined to feed me, isn't she?" he asked, grinning down at her, his unruly black hair tumbling across his tanned brow. "Between your mother and Miss Ruth, I'm going to look like a sumo wrestler."

Rebecca laughed. "Hardly. Of course, you could always go running with Daddy every morning."

Frank took a breath that shook his broad shoulders. "I think I get enough exercise on this job," he said, tossing a scrap of lumber on the waste heap. "I took your advice and reorganized my business," he told her. "It didn't set well with the boys."

"I'm sorry," Rebecca said contritely.

"It's not your fault," Frank told her, continuing to clean up the work site. "I just plunged into this whole thing without much forethought. Not very typical of me, I assure you. I go where I'm sent, but I do think about it. This all started with straightening up the churchyard and making a few repairs around the parish hall. Then I did some chores for Miss Ruth, and the business just escalated from there. Not very well planned, I admit, and not really accomplishing what I'd hoped."

"What was it supposed to do?" Rebecca asked.

"Just fill in a gap—until the parish is on a sounder footing that is."

Rebecca rested the seat of her cutoff jeans against the fender of his dusty pickup truck. "I probably should have left well enough alone," she said. "I have a tendency to say things and do things without working out all the details in my mind first."

"Well, we live by the truth, come when it will," Frank said philosophically.

"I've always been practical," Rebecca said. "Law does that to a person, and Mama has always kept a keen eye on budgets and that sort of thing. Then, living in a city like Atlanta, the dollar sign is always hung on everything. It's not like here. I never knew that I had more than other people did until I got my driver's license and Daddy gave me a car."

She interpreted the smile Frank gave her as saying *I should have known*.

Rebecca turned away from him and picked up a broom to sweep sawdust into a pile near the sawhorses Frank used when he cut lumber.

"You don't have to do that," Frank said, starting to take the broom from her hand.

"You want to get out of here before it starts to rain, don't you?"

"Out of the rain, perhaps," Frank said, wiping his hands on his carpenter's apron, "not necessarily out of your company."

When she looked up at him, a sudden uneasiness at his tone freezing her where she was, he put his hand under her chin and held it steady. His touch was gentle, but she felt a strength and warmth that she hadn't been prepared for, and in that moment she gasped for a breath that, when it came, was inadequate to settle the unsteadiness she felt.

In that instant she had to come to terms with the fact that Frank wasn't some ethereal being, that he had the substance of a flesh-and-blood person, and she had to come to terms with all that her realization entailed.

His dark eyes were questioning, but they held the fire that she'd seen before, and she recognized it as desire, long denied and controlled, no longer leashed and tamed.

Rebecca blinked against the wind, and when she opened her eyes again Frank's head was bending close to hers. His lips touched hers tentatively, then settled a gentle kiss on them.

But, as she touched him, unable to avoid placing her hand on his broad, muscular chest, Rebecca could feel the pounding of his heart, and she knew it matched her own. A sigh escaped her, unbidden.

A part of the gentleness of the kiss evaporated, and Rebecca felt the almost crushing force of Frank's longings. Before she could control her own reactions, she pressed herself against him, never giving a thought to the reserve that had always been part of her innermost being.

At that very moment, large drops of rain began spattering them, drumming rhythmically on the truck. Chilled by a breeze that touched nothing but her flushed face, Rebecca backed away from him and let him have the broom they'd both been clinging to.

"So much for—"

"This afternoon," Frank finished, tossing the broom easily into the back of the truck.

Curiosity, Rebecca thought, moving away from him. "Should I tell Mama you're coming to dinner?" she asked, walking backward toward the porch.

"Yes, and tell her thanks for asking me," Frank called, securing the tarpaulin over his tools. "I'm looking forward to it."

He meant more than he was saying with those words, and they both knew it. His dark eyes sent a flash across the distance between them, more disturbing than the lightning that arced across the sky, and his smile did serious damage to her attempt at maintaining her equilibrium.

Rebecca turned and dashed up the porch steps and into the house, her heart beating more heavily than it should have after so little exertion.

There had been several breaks in the storm, each one shorter than the last, and each shower had been heavier than the one preceding it.

"I hope the electricity doesn't go off," Margaret fretted as she put a pie into the oven. "Wouldn't that be awful?"

"We could just run over to the deli in the supermarket to get something for dinner," Rebecca said, then laughed at the horrified look on her mother's face.

"Feed company—a minister, no less—food I didn't fix myself!" Margaret exclaimed, sputtering. "Never! Rebecca Susanne Hobbs, how dare you even suggest such a thing!"

"Well—" Rebecca shrugged "—if worse comes to worst—"

"Put candles on the table," Margaret said. "There's a fresh set of pink ones in the drawer of the buffet."

Margaret had a certain priority system in her head, and Rebecca only sensed its workings. Thursday evening dinner, minister or not, didn't merit the lace tablecloth, or even the best damask linen. The second-best linen tablecloth was spread on the dining room table.

"We could eat in the kitchen," Rebecca suggested, then backed away, laughing. "Mama, don't go to so much trouble!"

"It's not trouble," Margaret countered, removing linen napkins from the buffet drawer. "It's just the proper way of doing things."

In turning back toward the table, Margaret dropped one of the napkins on the floor. "Oh—!" She was able to bite back the word she was going to say next, but her face colored, and her mouth set in a tight line.

Rebecca picked up the napkin and handed it back to her mother. "What's wrong, Mama?"

Margaret dusted off the napkin and put it precisely in place on the tablecloth. "Don't pay any attention to me," she said. "I'm just a little on edge."

"Mama, you've entertained judges and an ex-governor at this table, for heaven's sake! Frank is just a small-town minister who works as a handyman."

"That has nothing to do with it," Margaret said, stalking purposefully into the kitchen. "Nothing at all."

"Then what is it?" Rebecca asked, following her.

"It's your father," Margaret confessed, looking around the kitchen to decide what to attack next. "He's being...strange. He starts to talk to me and then just stops in the middle of what he's saying. The only time he ever acts like this is right before my birthday, and that's not for another three months."

"Well, maybe it has to do with one of his cases...."

"No, there's nothing on the docket he's having that much trouble with," Margaret said, bending down to check on the apple pie in the oven.

"Don't worry about it," Rebecca said. "I—I have to go take my bath, Mama."

"Wear a dress," Margaret called to her when Rebecca was halfway up the stairs.

"I'll see what I can come up with," Rebecca answered, glad she had thought of an excuse to get out of the kitchen. She'd been so close to telling her mother about Big Ted's chance at the federal bench that one more glance at the pain in Margaret's eyes would have overcome all the resolve in her soul.

Rebecca was amazed at her mother's resilience when she returned to the kitchen. Everything was in control, and Margaret was putting the finishing touches on a fruit salad, a bright smile on her face.

It had taken Rebecca longer to dress for dinner than she'd anticipated, and when her father drove into the yard she was surprised to see how late it was.

Margaret reacted with barely contained disappointment when she saw that Big Ted had not only his briefcase but also several manila folders with him. "I see you have to do some work tonight," she observed, hanging her oven mitts on a hook over the range.

"I'm afraid so."

"I think I'll go change for dinner," Margaret said, turning toward the back stairs.

"What's wrong?" Big Ted asked, starting toward his study to put down his armload of work.

"Mama asked Frank to dinner," Rebecca said, following him.

"Well, a little company for dinner doesn't usually put your mama into a swivet," Big Ted replied. "Come on. What's she upset about?"

"You," Rebecca said, keeping her voice low, knowing how sound carried in the old house. "She thinks you're avoiding her. Maybe lost interest in her."

"Well, you know what it's all about," Big Ted said, unloading his briefcase and arranging his files in some order on his desk.

"You're edgy about your federal appointment, and you still haven't told her about it," Rebecca said. "Daddy, I know you don't want to get her hopes up and then have her disappointed, but don't you see that she's fair enough to be disappointed with the system and not with you?"

"Honey, to me it would feel the same. The less said, the better," Big Ted said, tossing his briefcase in its usual place on a footstool. "Now, let me take a look at you. Um-hum! I think you'll do."

"What are you talking about?" Rebecca asked.

Big Ted just grinned back at her. "Look, I'd better go change for dinner myself. I'll try to patch things up with your mama, but when she gets this way she's hard to handle. Thank God I don't mess up too often."

Rebecca wandered back to the kitchen to keep a nervous eye on the meal her mother had left her in charge of by default. As the rain grew stronger, she went to the dining room to look out the front windows at the wet landscape beyond. When Frank drove up to the curb in his disreputable truck she hurried to the front door to meet him so that he wouldn't have to wait on the porch with the wind swirling rain under the protective overhang.

"Good evening," he said breathlessly as he passed her after wiping his feet cursorily on the jute welcome mat.

Rebecca wanted to reach out and brush the raindrops from his black hair as they glistened in the light from the hallway chandelier.

"It would turn nasty tonight, wouldn't it?" Rebecca asked, resisting the impulse. "I'll get you a towel—"

"Never mind," Frank said, dashing the drops from his hair with his own hand. "I won't melt."

"Mama and Daddy are still upstairs changing for dinner," Rebecca explained, "but I could get you a drink."

Frank looked back at her for a long moment, his dark eyes studying her, not in the blatantly sexual manner she was all too familiar with from the men in Atlanta, but as though he were trying to pierce the secrets of her very soul. Then he shook his head. "Well, lemonade or iced tea, perhaps."

"Come back to the kitchen and we'll see what we can find," Rebecca said.

In the kitchen Margaret was lifting her baked ham from the oven. "Good evening, Frank," she said, looking up from her work. Only Rebecca detected the tightness in her tone.

"Mama, is there some lemonade?"

"Yes, darlin', but Frank might prefer something stronger on a night like this," Margaret said.

"No, thank you, Miss Margaret," Frank said. "Lemonade sounds fine."

Rebecca poured two glasses of lemonade and handed one to Frank. "Mama, do you need any help?"

"No, no. Oh, go light the candles in the dining room, then sit down somewhere and rest."

Frank followed Rebecca into the dining room and stood by the window where Rebecca had watched for him. Now, though, she sensed that he was watching her. She blew out the match she'd lit the candles with and dropped it into an ashtray on the buffet.

THE JOKER GOES WILD!

Play
this
card
right!

See
inside!

SILHOUETTE®
WANTS TO <u>GIVE</u> YOU

- 4 free books
- A free bracelet watch
- A free mystery gift

IT'S A WILD, WILD, WONDERFUL

FREE OFFER!

HERE'S WHAT YOU GET:

1. *Four New Silhouette Romance™ Novels—FREE!* Everything comes up hearts and diamonds with four exciting romances—yours FREE from Silhouette Reader Service™. Each of these brand-new novels brings you the passion and tenderness of today's greatest love stories.

2. *A Practical and Elegant Bracelet Watch—FREE!* As a free gift simply to thank you for accepting four free books, we'll send you a stylish bracelet watch. This classic LCD quartz watch is a perfect expression of your style and good taste, and it's yours FREE as an added thanks for giving our Reader Service a try.

3. *An Exciting Mystery Bonus—FREE!* You'll go wild over this surprise gift. It is attractive as well as practical.

4. *Free Home Delivery!* Join Silhouette Reader Service™ and enjoy the convenience of previewing six new books every month, delivered to your home. Each book is yours for $2.25*. And there is *no* extra charge for postage and handling! If you're not fully satisfied, you can cancel at any time, just by sending us a note or a shipping statement marked "cancel" or by returning any shipment to us at our cost. Great savings and total convenience are the name of the game at Silhouette!

5. *Free Newsletter!* It makes you feel like a partner to the world's most popular authors . . . tells about their upcoming books . . . even gives you their recipes!

6. *More Mystery Gifts Throughout the Year!* No Joke! Because home subscribers are our most valued readers, we'll be sending you additional free gifts from time to time with your monthly shipments—as a token of our appreciation!

GO WILD
WITH SILHOUETTE® TODAY—
JUST COMPLETE, DETACH AND
MAIL YOUR FREE-OFFER CARD!

*Terms and prices subject to change without notice. NY and Iowa residents subject to sales tax.

© 1989 HARLEQUIN ENTERPRISES LIMITED

GET YOUR GIFTS FROM SILHOUETTE®
ABSOLUTELY FREE!

Mail this card today!

PLACE
JOKER
STICKER
HERE

PLAY THIS CARD RIGHT!

YES! Please send me my 4 Silhouette Romance™ novels FREE along with my free Bracelet Watch and free mystery gift. I wish to receive all the benefits of the Silhouette Reader Service™ as explained on the opposite page.

(U-S-R-12/89) 215 CIS HAYC

NAME _____
(PLEASE PRINT)

ADDRESS _____ APT. _____

CITY _____

STATE _____ ZIP CODE _____

Offer limited to one per household and not valid to current Silhouette Romance subscribers. All orders subject to approval.

SILHOUETTE BOOKS
"NO RISK" GUARANTEE

- There's no obligation to buy—and the free books remain yours to keep.
- You don't pay for postage and handling and receive books before they appear in stores.
- You may end your subscription anytime—just write and let us know or return any shipment to us at our cost.

IT'S NO JOKE!

MAIL THE POSTPAID CARD AND GET FREE GIFTS AND $9.00 WORTH OF SILHOUETTE NOVELS—FREE!

"I didn't know you would be so formal," Frank said.

"Aunt Ruth never was one to put herself out once the pot had boiled," Rebecca said with a laugh. "But she's a great cook."

Frank nodded. "She's comfortable to be around," he said.

"Oh, I hope we're not putting you at a disadvantage," Rebecca said, moving slightly toward him. "You seem perfectly at ease, no matter what." Somehow she'd gotten the impression that he wasn't the least out of his element with her mother's style of hospitality.

Frank's jaw flexed, but he didn't say anything. Rebecca sensed that she wouldn't easily find out anything about the background of this man she was so attracted to.

Her father came into the dining room, carrying a drink in his hand—something that was out of character for him—and reached out to shake Frank's hand.

"Big Ted," Frank said, a note of apology in his voice, "this rain is playing rough with the schedule for getting the work done."

"Don't worry about something you can't control," Big Ted said. "You don't control the weather, do you?" he asked skeptically.

"No, sir, I don't. But the garage is all sealed in."

"Then don't worry," Big Ted said, taking a sip of his drink. "Ah, Margaret! Do you need some help with that platter?"

"You all go in the parlor while I clear the table," Margaret said when the apple pie had been reduced to a few flaky crumbs and the lingering scent of cinnamon. "I'll make a pot of coffee. It'll taste good on a night like this."

"None for me," Big Ted said, getting to his feet. "I have some papers to look over before I get too involved in a baseball game tonight."

"Mama, I'll help you," Rebecca said.

"No, no, you and Frank go relax," Margaret insisted.

Rebecca started toward the front parlor, and Frank gladly followed her, relieved that dinner was over and he no longer needed to weigh every word he said, every move he made, every glance he sent in Rebecca's direction.

"She gets this way sometimes," Rebecca said softly. "I hope you don't mind being shunted off to the parlor."

"If you want to know the truth," Frank said slowly, surveying the formally decorated parlor, with its velvet settees and its plush carpeting, "I've been looking forward to being alone with you all afternoon."

"Why, Reverend Andrews!" Rebecca said in her mocking drawl. "Ah had no ah-deah!"

Frank laughed and turned toward the oil landscape over the marble fireplace.

"That's a local scene, done by one of Mama's friends," Rebecca explained. She was standing so close that he was tempted to reach out to her, but she moved much too quickly. When he turned away from the painting, she was gazing out the window at the rain.

The silence between them was filled with the growing intensity of the storm outside.

"How much longer will you be in Blakesley Hills?" he asked her.

"I'd planned to go back to Atlanta tomorrow," she told him. "But there are a few unresolved things here at home I want to see through."

"I hope you don't take this the wrong way," Frank said, coming to stand close behind her. "But I've been looking forward to talking to you. It's been a long time since I've just . . . talked to someone. I'm either preaching or teaching or trying to accomplish something. And I'm tired of it. I've wanted to talk to someone with whom I can put aside my job and just be myself. I sense I can do that with you. I hope I'm not wrong."

Stunned, Rebecca stared at him for a long moment. "I . . . I do think I know what you mean," she said. "There are times when I feel all I am is a legal-advice machine. There is no one in the company where I—where I work—that's a friend. The women who are secretaries and clerks don't seem to see me as one of them, and of course the men don't share anything with me, and I'd never presume to get too close to anyone who's married."

"I can see that would be a problem," Frank said. "I can't even be myself with the Blakesley boys. I feel as though I have to maintain a certain element of authority with them."

The telephone rang twice, and Rebecca started toward the hallway, but she was barely out the door when it stopped. Her mother had probably answered it. Rebecca retraced her steps and was about to sit down on one of the settees when she heard her mother coming down the hall.

"Frank, I hate to bother you, but it's my sister Ruth," Margaret said, concern in her voice. "She said it's very important."

Frank sighed and followed her. "Yes, Miss Ruth?" he asked.

"Have you seen the Blakesley boys in the last few hours?" she asked over a line snapping with static.

"No, I haven't seen them since about one o'clock, just before the first shower this afternoon. Why?"

"Wanda Blakesley just called, and she's frantic. She thinks they've run away!"

"*They what?* How can she be sure?"

"Their bikes and their backpacks are gone, and they rarely miss a meal, no matter how angry they are. They were supposed to be at a ballgame, but she called one of the coaches and discovered it had been rained out. Where do you think they would go?"

"Let me think," Frank said, running his hand through his hair.

"You know, this will make Big Ted very angry with them. Can we keep it from him?"

"No, I'll have to tell him. Tell Mrs. Blakesley I'll do what I can."

Rebecca was on her feet when he returned to the parlor. "What happened?"

"Mrs. Blakesley called Miss Ruth. The boys seem to have run away!" Frank told her. *This is all I need,* he thought in frustration. *The first chance I have to be alone with Rebecca and they mess it up.*

"I don't believe it!" Rebecca exclaimed. The look she gave him was a reflection of the frustration he felt inside. "Any idea how long they've been gone?"

"There was supposed to be a baseball game this afternoon that they wanted to watch at the Legion field, but it was called off and they haven't come home."

"I assume they have their bikes," Rebecca said.

"They could be anywhere by now," Frank said.

"No, they can only be in one place," Rebecca said. "All we have to do is find them."

"Your father will have their hides," Frank said, lowering his voice.

"Well, we'll just have to try to keep it from him," Rebecca told him. "It's not impossible."

Margaret came into the hallway. "What's wrong?"

"Mama, I need to borrow your car," Rebecca said, taking control of the situation.

"Well, of course, but why?"

Rebecca decided to take Margaret into their confidence. "The Blakesley twins are missing—on their bikes—and we're going out to look for them."

"In this mess?" Margaret asked, just as thunder rumbled in the distance.

"Keep the coffee hot," Rebecca said, snatching her mother's keys from the desk in the hall and heading through the kitchen to the laundry room.

Donning one of the family rain slickers and motioning Frank to take the other one, she grabbed the beach towels, an umbrella and a flashlight. Margaret's organization was there for a reason, Rebecca reflected.

"We'll start looking from their house," Rebecca said, backing her mother's station wagon out of the garage.

Blakesley Hills was an easy town to get around in. General Blakesley had laid it out in a grid, with streets named for heroes going north and south, and east and west streets named for trees and shrubs. His mansion had been built at the eastern limit of the town as he'd laid it out, at the corner of Oglethorpe and Peach.

The mansion was lit up in the gathering gloom of the stormy twilight. Frank and Rebecca dashed through the rain to the shelter of the big front veranda and were greeted by the distraught young Mrs. Blakesley almost before they rang the bell.

Wanda Blakesley, her blond hair disheveled and her clothing rumpled, led them into the foyer of the house, clearly upset and concerned, both about the boys' safety and about their father's reaction to the situation.

Frank asked all the questions: How long had the boys been gone? What were they wearing? Could they have gone to someone's home?

"You know, they haven't made any friends here yet," Mrs. Blakesley explained. "That's why I thought they might have gone over to Miss Ruth's to talk to you. That's why I called there."

"Well, we'll try to find them," Frank said.

"I just want them to be here before their father gets home from Augusta," Mrs. Blakesley said. "I don't want any more battles."

"Can I ask something?" Rebecca interjected, not wanting to hear any more about the family's problems when every moment was valuable. "How much money did they have at their disposal?"

Mrs. Blakesley shrugged. "Probably quite a lot. They're both . . . frugal with their allowances."

"Ah!" Rebecca said, turning toward the station wagon. "Let's go. I have a plan."

"What is it?" Frank asked, yelling to be heard above the heightening storm.

Rebecca scrambled into the car and slammed the door, quickly turning the key and easing the car along the sweeping circular drive in front of the Blakesley mansion. "Let's start with the baseball field over by the elementary school. There's a cement-block concession stand there where they might be holed up."

Frank mopped rain from his face with one of the towels Rebecca had brought along. "Assuming they even actually went to the game. They might have realized that it would be rained out. They might have just lit out for somewhere. They'd have a four-hour start on us."

"Maybe so," Rebecca said. "But I'm counting on two things. One, that they're smart enough to get in out of the rain, and two, that they'll react true to form and start arguing with each other about what they should do. If they do that, they'll slow down and we can catch them."

Frank chuckled. "How do you know things like that?"

"Elementary, my dear," she said with a laugh.

Rebecca eased the car along Oglethorpe Street toward the baseball field. The parking lot was a quagmire of wet red clay as her headlamps swept over it. She turned toward the concession stand, lonely and deserted in the darkness.

"They don't appear to be here," Frank said. "Should I get out and look?"

Rebecca didn't answer right away. The headlights were lighting the log that protected the concession stand from cars, and to her embarrassment she recognized the crude childish carving on it. Buddy Joe + Becca Su.

"What do you think?" Frank asked.

"Oh! They're not here," Rebecca said, startled by the question. "There's not enough room for two boys and their bikes in there without our being able to see them."

She threw the car into reverse, glad when the headlights swung away from the graffiti on the log.

"I assume Becca Su is a common name around here," Frank said when the silence of the car grew oppressive.

"Yes," Rebecca said. But she knew exactly who the artwork referred to. "I think the next place to check would be the pond."

"Pond?" Frank asked, easily diverted.

"We have a picnic grove with a big pavilion," Rebecca told him. "I think it's the nearest logical place to look."

"Why did you ask Mrs. Blakesley about how much money the boys might have?" Frank asked. He stretched his arm out along the back of the car seat, tapping the upholstery behind her left shoulder in a dull rhythm.

"Well, I was thinking they might have thought they could get a bus," she told him. "But they'd have to go—Gee, I can't even remember where the closest place is to get a bus."

Frank scowled at her. "Not exactly a comforting possibility."

She drove slowly into the park, along the lane that wound through pine trees and overgrown azaleas.

The pavilion wasn't as big as she remembered, and as luck would have it she parked right by a bench that was carved with the legend J.T. + R.S.H. Well, there was no getting around that one, was there?

Rebecca stared at the crude letters while Frank surveyed the pavilion. There was a relatively dry area in the middle of the shelter, but the place was empty of anything but pop cans, potato-chip bags and dried pine needles.

She must have sat staring a moment too long, because Frank got impatient.

"Carving initials must be a favorite sport around here," he said, shifting his long legs and tapping his feet on the tread in front of him.

"Oh, the young men are regular cutups," Rebecca quipped. "Let's just drive through town and see if they're holed up at the Crispy Cone or somewhere."

Frank was displaying some impatient mannerisms that were beginning to get on her nerves.

"Has it been awfully rainy this summer?" Rebecca asked as they left the park.

"No, this seems unusual, to hear people talk," Frank said. "Where I'd been, we had rain almost every day."

Rebecca turned toward a side street where she knew there was an abandoned house. "I hear you had problems with tropical diseases," she said.

"Um..." Frank responded. "As much as I liked what I was doing, my body just couldn't take the heat and all the germs. My superior kept trying to tell me I should go back home, but it wasn't until I heard a little voice saying that He hadn't spent five years pushing me into the ministry to lose me to malaria that I agreed to be reassigned."

"Malaria?" Rebecca asked, concerned.

"Everything up until then was child's play."

Rebecca gaped at the lot where the abandoned house should have been. It was now a parking lot for a day-care center in the house next door. Scratch one more hiding place. She moved on toward the courthouse square.

"This weather can't help you very much," Rebecca said. "Getting soaked Tuesday night and then again tonight."

"I'm all right, though," Frank said. "I've got some medication back at my room in case I go into chills."

"That's good to know," Rebecca said flatly, trying to see into the cars parked around the Crispy Cone, the longtime hangout of the kids in Blakesley Hills. She drove behind the building, careful to ease the car over the speed bump.

She breathed a sigh of relief when she saw that sometime in the past seven years the whole building had been repainted. There was no trace of the heart that had been spray-painted on the fence that hid the garbage cans.

"Well, that's it," Frank said with a dejected sigh as she turned back onto the street.

"Not by a long shot," Rebecca told him. "Tim and Jim have to be somewhere, and I have to think they're too smart to tackle the wet roads in this filthy weather."

They were stopped at the town's one traffic light when it came to her. She circled the block and went back the way they'd come, then took a turn down a dirt road. The car bounced from one pothole to another.

"Where on earth are you taking me?" Frank asked bracing himself with one hand on the dashboard in front of him.

"I think I know where the boys are!" Rebecca assured him. "They bike everywhere, don't they?"

"Yes."

"Well, I'm counting on them knowing about this place."

They went over a set of railroad tracks that made the well-built car creak, then turned into the weed-sprouted yard of a deserted rail depot.

"This is it?" Frank asked skeptically.

"This is my best guess," Rebecca said, keeping her voice low, as if the boys would be able to hear in this driving rain.

"This looks like a big place," Frank observed, adjusting his slicker.

"There's only one section of good roof, though, and I came in the back way, so they might not have seen us." Rebecca handed him the umbrella and searched for the flashlight.

"How can you be so sure they'll be here?" he asked, pausing before he opened the car door.

"I'm not," she said, pushing open the door and wishing belatedly that she'd taken the time to change her shoes. "It's just the best guess I can make at the moment."

She switched on the flashlight and motioned for Frank to follow her as she moved cautiously around to the side of the building closest to the disused paved road.

"This used to be a really busy place, I'm told, back when they shipped grain and cotton by rail. Now everything goes by truck."

Walking so close to her that their raincoats occasionally scraped together, Frank tried to shield her with the umbrella. "If you ask me," Frank said in a low whisper, "it looks like it's still a pretty busy place."

"Well, everybody likes to leave his mark," Rebecca said softly.

Turning the corner of the building, Rebecca shone her flashlight on an old double door that had long since lost all hope of closing. Ignoring the blue splashes that proclaimed

Animal loves Reba, she slipped inside and nearly tripped over a bicycle.

She turned to give Frank an I-told-you-so smile as he followed her. When she looked back, her flashlight picked up the shapes of two boys huddled by another bike, clutching their backpacks and shielding their eyes from the light.

"Okay, boys," Frank said firmly. "You've ruined a perfectly wonderful evening. What do you have to say for yourselves?"

Chapter Seven

Sheesh!"

"Cripes!"

Jim turned to Tim in the darkness. "You said no one would find us here."

Rebecca moved the beam of the flashlight so that it no longer blinded the twins but reflected off a wall. "You didn't know you were up against a native," she said.

"Come on, boys," Frank said, furling the umbrella and reaching out to clamp a hand on one boy's shoulder. "Let's go back home."

"No!" the boy said, wrenching away from Frank.

They struggled, but Frank got hold of them both. "Pick up your bikes and take them out to the car."

"No!"

"You can't stay here all night," Rebecca said, trying to reason with them. "It's a miserable place even in good weather. Come on, boys. We need to talk, and this is no place for a long conversation."

The boys conferred with each other in a shorthand of grunts and gestures that Rebecca couldn't begin to decipher, but after a few moments they shook Frank's hands away, squared their shoulders and picked up their bikes.

"Where's the car?" one of them asked.

"Around the side of the building," Frank said.

Rebecca picked up their backpacks, scooted ahead of them to light the way and opened the back of the station wagon to let them stow their bicycles. The boys were muttering to each other, and she sensed that a rebellion was brewing.

"Get in, fellas," she told them firmly. "There are some towels there."

Frank got in the front on the passenger side and passed towels to the boys as they settled in the back. Rebecca found the ignition key in the unsteady glow of the dome light, then glanced around before slamming the door closed. "Everybody ready?" she asked.

"Ready as we'll ever be," one of the boys muttered.

Frank braced himself and sneezed, wiped the rain from his face and sneezed again.

Rebecca started the car, switched on the windshield wipers and the headlights, then studied Frank's face in the light from the instrument panel.

"You're getting the chills, aren't you?" she asked, in a voice that was barely loud enough for him to hear over the slap of the wipers.

"No," he answered.

"I thought preachers didn't lie," Rebecca said, putting the car in gear.

Frank stiffened and set his jaw grimly. He sneezed again.

"Guys," Rebecca said, leaning back and turning her head to the side, "I was going to take you straight home, but I've got to get Frank someplace warm and dry right away, which means my place.''

One of the boys piped up. ''Hey, it can't be any worse than home.''

''You have to realize what you're getting into there,'' Rebecca cautioned. ''My father's home.''

''We messed up. We'll take the heat,'' one of the boys mumbled.

She drove through the rain, glad that the car was reliable and wasn't about to leave them stranded in the storm.

As they came over a hill and under an old railroad trestle, the headlights illuminated yet another example of juvenile art. Reba—Marry me!—C.

Her face flushed in the darkness.

''No wonder your mother's on the beautification project,'' Frank muttered.

Several remarks came to Rebecca's mind, but none of them seemed appropriate.

The porch lights of the Hobbs house were all glowing as Rebecca drew into the drive. She pulled as close to the house as possible and motioned for everyone to get out. ''Just leave the bikes where they are,'' she said. ''I'll put the car in the garage and be in in a minute.''

A strange car was parked in the turnaround, a sleek silver sport coupe shiny in the rain. ''There's Dad's car,'' one of the boys grumbled.

''The knee-cruncher.''

When she entered the house, angry voices were already echoing through the hallway outside Big Ted's study. An empty coffee carafe in her hand, Margaret stood outside the closed door, her brow furrowed and her lips in a thin line.

''What happened?'' Rebecca asked, shrugging out of her raincoat and pushing her damp hair out of her eyes.

"The colonel got home just after you left the Blakesleys'," Margaret explained, "and they came over here to talk to your father."

"I was hoping Daddy wouldn't know about this," Rebecca said, lowering her voice, "but I guess it was unavoidable. Frank needs something hot to drink." She started into the kitchen and reached for the kettle on the stove.

"I'll take care of that, dear," Margaret said, taking the kettle from her hand. "You see if you can keep everyone from coming to blows."

Rebecca took a deep breath and squared her shoulders. With long strides she barged into the study.

"...can't possibly enter them in school if they're..."

"...military prep school will straighten them out..."

"...run away every chance we can get!"

"...have done everything I can think of..."

"...boys can't be trusted out of our sight..."

"...can't even trust a preacher..."

Rebecca took one look at the scene and tucked her lowered lip between her teeth. A piercing whistle rent the air, and suddenly all eyes swung in her direction.

Frank's face was ashen, and his hands were trembling as he clutched the back of the nearest chair.

"Frank, Mama wants you in the kitchen," she said firmly. "Mrs. Blakesley, Colonel, good evening."

She was just assuming he was the colonel; he looked like every Blakesley she'd ever known—blond, stocky and autocratic. If he was anything like the rest of the family, it would take a lot for her to learn to like him.

"My daughter Rebecca," Big Ted said, belatedly introducing her to the Blakesleys. "Reba had a few years of experience in youth advocacy during law school," he went on. "She knows quite a lot about—things like this."

"Hmmm." Colonel Blakesley said, grudgingly extending a hand toward her.

"Look, everybody," Rebecca said, glancing from the boys' bedraggled jeans to the grim looks they were getting from three pairs of eyes, "I have a suggestion. It's been my experience that nothing constructive ever comes of a confrontation like this. It's best if all sides draw back, take some time to get control of their tempers, think over what they've done to cause this problem and what they are willing to contribute to a solution. Let's all step back and cool off for a while. I suggest that you let me take the boys home in my car so no one says anything that can't be taken back later. I'll meet with the boys here tomorrow morning and talk with them, and then I'll get back to each of you—the way we negotiated when I was working in advocacy. Is that agreeable to everyone?"

Heads nodded, some more readily than others. The boys, however, seemed uncertain about going home.

"Come on, let's get going," Rebecca said. "I'll take you home in my car. You can get the bikes tomorrow."

She turned to the less attractive job of pinning down the colonel and his wife to an appointment the next day and arranged to meet them at the country club the next afternoon.

Frank entered the kitchen gingerly, grasping the doorjamb until his eyes got used to the strong overhead light. "Rebecca told me that you wanted to speak to me," he said tentatively.

Margaret turned from pouring steaming water into a small teapot, a smile coming to her lips. Her eyes looked a bit guilty. "She used to get her brother Donnie out of the way with that old line." Margaret chuckled. "Actually, she thought you needed a little hot tea and a sit-down." Margaret put down the kettle and reached out to touch his fore-head with a gentle hand. "I think she's right. We'll just nip this in the bud. Sit down right here. The tea will be ready in a minute."

At that moment Frank's body made the decision for him, and he sat down on a ladder-back chair that was between the door and the range. "Yes," he said, sighing. "Why do things like this always happen on rainy nights? I went through the same thing Tuesday, when I got back to Ruth's after being here."

"That's what Ruth told me," Margaret said, stirring the contents of the teapot with one hand and reaching for a heavy crockery mug with the other. "I'm afraid you won't be able to keep many secrets so long as you live with Ruth. Not that she's a gossip, but she's very concerned with people's welfare. We'll have you fixed up in a minute."

Frank slumped back in the chair, watching without comprehension as Margaret poured the amber liquid into the mug and laced it heavily with lemon and honey. He could almost taste the tea in his throat already, knowing it wasn't going to be the politely tepid, barely colored concoction he'd suffered through at, say, a bishop's reception.

He liked Margaret's attitude toward him. She wasn't being deferential or patronizing. She would probably treat her own son the way she was treating him. That was comforting.

He wrapped his hands around the mug when she handed it to him, absorbing the warmth through almost trembling fingers.

"Can I do anything else for you?" Margaret asked. "Are you warm enough?"

"Yes, thank you," he said, blowing on the tea. The tea burned his tongue, but after a moment he felt calmer.

The study was quiet, with just a murmur of voices now and again. He was glad he wasn't in the room with the boys, because he was temporarily out of patience with them, and he was ashamed of himself for feeling as he did. He'd made great strides toward changing those of his own attitudes that were unbecoming for a minister, but there were times when he slipped back into the impetuousness of his youth.

"Where did you find the boys?" Margaret asked, turning a kitchen chair around so that she could face him.

"At a railroad depot out in the country," Frank told her.

"Out at Old Kerry? That's a likely place to run away to."

"We looked in several places before we went there."

"Rebecca knows the country as well as anyone, I suppose," Margaret said with a little laugh.

Frank looked at her for a long moment, then took another swallow of tea. "We checked the ball field, a picnic pavilion, the Crispy Cone, and another place where Rebecca thought they might be, but now it's just an empty lot. Then she drove out to the depot by way of a dirt road as though she knew they would be there. I must say, I was impressed."

Margaret leaned an elbow on the table. "Rebecca tends to rise to difficult situations. Sometimes I think she thrives on disaster."

He felt his mouth quirking up in a smile. Since he'd been sent to Central America and seen a life remote from what he was used to, he'd lost some of the objectivity he needed to cope at times. At least he hadn't become insensitive, he thought, trying to console himself, but he did let things get to him.

"Well, maybe she was able to come through because she wasn't as close to the problem as the Blakesleys and I are," Frank said. "It's truly frightening to see boys that age ruining their own lives."

"Some parents, particularly daddies, don't know how much their children need their approval," Margaret sighed. "The Blakesleys in particular. Keep in mind...I've lived here all my life except for my college days. I know everything about everybody. The Blakesleys have always packed their boys off to military prep schools around thirteen or fourteen years of age and let someone else discipline them. I'm not disputing that they have become fine, upstanding military officers. But I think it has also cheated the boys out of a stage of development of knowing their daddies as their equals, as well as their superiors."

Frank studied Margaret for a long moment while he thought over what she'd just said. She got up slowly, refilled his mug and sat down again.

The door to the study opened, and Frank heard people moving around.

"No, just leave the bikes in Mama's car," Rebecca said, apparently overruling a suggestion. "I'm holding them as security that you boys will show up here tomorrow at nine o'clock. You aren't getting those bikes back until we have a long talk and get a few things settled."

"Aw, shucks," one of the boys said.

"There's nothing that can't be negotiated," Rebecca assured him. "It's just that we aren't going to start negotiating until we've all had some time to cool off."

Big Ted came into the kitchen. "Ah! Tea! I think I'll have a cup myself," he said, reaching for a mug. "Anyone else?"

"No, thank you," Colonel Blakesley said. "We're going straight home."

"I'll bring the boys along in a moment," Rebecca promised him, reaching for her raincoat.

Big Ted looked down at Frank, then reached out to detain his daughter. "Stop by Ruth's place on your way home.

I think I'll ride over there with Frank to see that she's all right.''

Frank smiled at the way the Hobbses took care of the people around them, making it look as though nothing at all were wrong. Big Ted probably didn't think he could drive two blocks while he had a chill, so he would most likely offer to drive.

But the excuse was that he wanted to see if Ruth was all right. And Ruth was sturdy as an ox, being of the same gene pool that had produced Margaret and Rebecca, two women whom very little fazed.

There was a respite from the rain when Rebecca delivered Tim and Jim to the Blakesley home. Most of the way there they'd been taciturn and remote, but Rebecca didn't feel any hostility directed toward her. Maybe counseling them was going to work.

They were polite enough when they thanked her for the ride home, but it was plain that they were a little baffled as to why she'd insisted on giving them the ride when they could just as well have ridden home with their father. But she wanted to buffer them from the emotions she'd sensed radiating from the colonel.

She would have to talk with Colonel Blakesley, and she wasn't too anxious to confront him. He was the type of man who'd made up his mind when he was six months old and had never changed it for anything.

She parked the car in front of Aunt Ruth's house and sat there for a moment, wondering what to do. Well, it wasn't polite to just sit there waiting for Big Ted to come out. Aunt Ruth would be insulted.

Rebecca slipped in the front door—after all, she was family—into the living room of Ruth's homey little place.

Somewhere, probably in the kitchen, Ruth and Big Ted were talking in hushed tones.

"Daddy, I'm here," Rebecca called softly, barely raising her voice.

"I'll be right there, honey," Big Ted answered, but she heard no footsteps on the usually creaky floor.

Frank came down the last few steps into the living room, a faded sweatshirt having replaced the black knit shirt he'd worn earlier.

"Are you all right?" she asked him anxiously.

Frank nodded. "I have to say, I was a bit miffed with you earlier, but you did the right thing. You kept me from falling on my face and looking like a—"

Rebecca stopped him by grasping his arm. "You're not that hung up on appearances, are you?" she asked.

"I know I shouldn't be," he said, trying for a lighter tone. "But I'm not perfect. Although I'm still working at it," he said after a pause.

"Well, I've never really tried." Rebecca chuckled. "Look, I know what you must be thinking of me. The girl most likely to inspire graffiti in Blakesley Hills."

Frank's dark eyes softened in the reflected light of the shaded lamps in Aunt Ruth's parlor. "It's really none of my business," he said, but the hands clasping hers had an anxious pressure to them that belied his words.

"It was like having my life flash before my eyes," Rebecca quipped, "driving around and seeing those . . . those sentiments splashed all over everywhere. But you have to realize that they span a long period of time. Young guys tend to get a little carried away with their jackknives and spray cans—more than a relationship might warrant."

"You mean C wasn't really serious about marrying you when he hung by his heels over the rail of the railroad trestle?" Frank asked.

"Well, I certainly never asked him to do such a thing!" Rebecca said defensively.

"To be honest," Frank said softly, bending his head down so that his lips were close to her ear, "I would have been surprised if you hadn't had some of the experiences of a typical young lady. You're much too pretty for any boy— or man—to ignore."

Rebecca looked at his piercing dark eyes for a long moment. "You shock me," she said, her throat barely letting the words out.

"Don't be caught up in the mystique of the collar," Frank told her, backing away slightly but still holding on to her hands. "I'm a man, as well as a minister. Every once in a while, like tonight, my humanity reaches out and grabs me a little more than I want it to. I don't mean the weakness of the malaria giving me the chills. I mean the anger at the boys and the...the jealousy of knowing someone else cared enough about you to whittle your name somewhere. With the jealousy came the knowledge that I care about you, and I'm not quite prepared for that right now."

Rebecca withdrew one of her hands from his clasp. "Why, shame on you for trifling with me this afternoon when you didn't know your own feelings!"

"Oh, I knew my feelings then," Frank told her. "It's just that now I know them even better." He bent forward and kissed her cheek gently.

Rebecca drew a quick breath and tried to understand what was happening. To her, ministers were usually older men who lived very proper and circumspect existences. Sure, they had wives, but she'd never given any thought to their love lives.

Frank drew her close and kissed her again, capturing her lips with his. It wasn't unexpected. Nor was the excitement that seared Rebecca's soul unwelcome. It was just the moment that made her cautious.

She backed off, feeling her face flush and trying to get control of her breathing. "Oh, my goodness," she said under her breath.

Rebecca heard her father's footsteps in the kitchen and decided that it was time to leave.

"I hope you don't mind that I want to talk with the boys tomorrow morning," Rebecca said in what approximated her normal voice.

"No, I plan to stay in and work on my sermon until the ground dries out enough that we can work in someone's yard," Frank told her.

"I—I thought the situation needed a disinterested party, a new perspective," Rebecca said. "Someone who was on the boys' side."

"I understand," Frank said. "I'll see you later, then."

Big Ted entered the living room. "Becca, you ready to go home?" he asked, tugging the collar of his windbreaker up around his neck.

"Yes, Daddy. Aunt Ruth, we haven't had a good visit since I've been home."

"I understand you've been right busy, young lady," Aunt Ruth said. Her glance included Frank, and Rebecca turned toward the door to hide the color she felt rising in her cheeks.

"She's afraid you'll put her to work on the church quilt," Big Ted teased.

"I already have," Aunt Ruth said with a laugh. "You take care now."

Rebecca dashed through the rain and started the car. Big Ted settled into the passenger seat and braced himself as he always did when he rode with Rebecca. It was probably a holdover from the year he'd taught her to drive.

"You did the right thing, Rebecca, stepping in like that. Even I was out of patience with those boys," he admitted.

Rebecca bit her lower lip. "They are a challenge, that's for sure."

"And what about Frank?"

"I hope he'll be all right," she said. "He looked better than when we were driving back from Old Kerry." She shook her head. "Every time we turned a corner there was some piece of artwork with my name on it!"

Big Ted laughed. "You did have a colorful youth, didn't you?"

Rebecca thought it best to leave that without comment.

Rebecca hurried down the back stairs to the kitchen, a lightness in her step that hadn't been there for ages, it seemed. The solution to the problem of what to do with Mrs. Gruber's house had popped into her mind when she'd opened her eyes. And she was looking forward to talking to the Blakesley twins to see if her theory about their problems was correct.

"There's coffee and melon," Margaret told her distractedly, checking through her purse. "Oh! You had my car last. What did you do with the keys?"

"I left them in the ignition, Mama," Rebecca told her cheerfully.

Margaret made a face and closed her purse. "No wonder I can't find them, then."

"Where are you going so early?" Rebecca asked, glancing at the clock above the refrigerator.

"The beauty shop," Margaret told her, taking one last swallow of her coffee and pouring the rest down the sink. "I'll be back around ten."

She was out the back door and across the porch before Rebecca had poured her coffee, and she was probably halfway to Jackson Street before Rebecca remembered that the twins' bicycles were still in the station wagon.

Rebecca made a hopeless gesture and sank her spoon into the cantaloupe she'd found in the refrigerator. She was in too good a mood for such a small thing to bother her.

The doorbell rang before she was finished with her breakfast. Tim and Jim Blakesley stood, identically respectful, on the front porch.

"Come in," Rebecca said, standing aside to let them in. 'You're early. I like that."

"Always early," Jim said, looking around the hallway.

"Mom always said we were early in the morning, early in the week and six weeks early altogether," Tim said.

Rebecca laughed, and they both turned wide blue eyes toward her, as though they were surprised by her reaction. "I'm not finished with my breakfast yet," she said, leading the way into the kitchen. "Would you like something? Toast? Coffee?"

The boys consulted each other with a look.

"Coffee?" Tim asked.

"There's plenty. Help yourselves," Rebecca said, motioning toward the counter and resuming her seat. "Make yourselves comfortable."

After fixing mugs of coffee, they took seats opposite her and watched her for a long moment.

"Well?" Tim asked.

"Suppose you tell me why you chose to run away on such an awful night," Rebecca suggested. "I mean, it didn't show a lot of planning on your part."

Jim leaned his elbows on the table and turned to Tim as though he expected him to explain. Tim pushed his coffee mug an inch farther away from him and took a deep breath.

"It was spur-of-the-moment. Not well thought out at all."

"Then something must have made you awfully mad at someone in a hurry," Rebecca observed.

"Yeah. Frank. We trusted him. Then he pulled that on us."

"Just like everybody else," Jim said. "He told us one thing, then did something else."

"Grown-ups are always doing that to us."

"We've been promised all sorts of things, but nothing ever comes out right. We thought we could trust Frank, though. A minister! Sheesh!"

"Aha!" Rebecca said. "That's what I thought. Look, guys, I'm sort of to blame for part of this. When I heard what Frank was charging for the work he was doing for my father, I told him he wasn't charging enough. We went over the way he figures his fees, and he was shortchanging himself and paying you guys much more than your work is really worth."

The boys stared at her.

"So you really should be mad at me," Rebecca said. Her words were greeted by a heavy silence.

"All right," she said, getting up from the table. "Come into the study, and I'll show you why he has to make some other arrangement to pay you, and how it could be to your advantage."

Tim was definitely skeptical, but Jim was willing to give her a chance, she sensed. She cleared her father's desk, took out a calculator, paper and pencils and sat down to explain a simple formula for running a small business. Soon they were punching numbers into the calculator and scribbling away on the paper, trying to adjust figures.

"If you assume the overhead for the truck and the mower is—" Rebecca was interrupted by the telephone in the hallway. "Darn! Can you guys just hold that thought while I answer the phone?"

Tim nodded and bent over the paper in front of him. The avid interest that lit his eyes matched that which had been kindled a few moments before in Jim.

"This is Thelma," Mrs. Pettigrew said excitedly.

"I'm sorry, Mama's not here," Rebecca said.

"I know! I want to talk to you, dear," Thelma said. "My husband just got a call from the president of ERM Properties, and I heard that you paid the taxes on Mrs. Gruber's place and got the deed. You clever child!"

"I thought it was clever at the time that I did it," Rebecca said with a laugh. "It's taken me a couple days to figure out what I'm going to do with it. I'll have to run over to the law library at the courthouse this morning to see how I can sign the house over to the restoration society to be used as a museum after Mrs. Gruber no longer needs it."

"What a marvelous idea! But I don't know if we can handle it."

"I thought I'd check everything out through the books and then get back to the restoration society," Rebecca said.

"Rebecca, darling, I just thought of something," Thelma said. "How would it be if I called an emergency board meeting for this afternoon at your place. You get everything in order to explain it to us, and we can talk about it before you go back to Atlanta."

Funny. It had been days since Rebecca had even thought of Atlanta. The word hit her. Yes, she would have to go back sometime, probably soon.

"That sounds like a good idea," Rebecca told her. "Mama should be back by ten. Call her when you've reached everyone, and she'll see that there is plenty of tea for us."

When she turned back toward the study, the boys were both standing in the door, watching her.

"You're going to make it into a museum?" Tim asked.

"Creepy Mrs. Gruber's place?"

"Mrs. Gruber is not creepy." Rebecca said.

"We meant the house," Jim told her.

"Great place for Halloween!" Tim said.

They followed her back to the desk. "Where were we?" Rebecca asked. "Oh. Overhead."

"Hm!" Tim said when they'd gone through another batch of figures. "We need to think some more."

"So now you understand why Frank did what he did," Rebecca said. "Now, fellas, I think you heard that I have to get over to the law library to work out what I'm going to do with Mrs. Gruber's house before the ladies come this afternoon. I'm sorry Mama got away before I thought to get the bikes out of her car. If you'll come back later, she'll let you have them."

"That's all you wanted with us?" Tim asked.

"No," Rebecca said. "But it's enough for now."

"Frank, the boys are here," Miss Ruth called softly from the bottom of the stairs. "Can you see them, or should I tell them to come back later?"

Frank drew a line through what he'd just written and dropped the pen on top of the yellow pad. "I'll be down," he said, pushing his bare feet into a pair of leather sandals he'd brought back from the tropics.

Tim and Jim got up from the glider on the porch when the screen door slammed, and Frank squinted against the bright sunshine. "Well, guys, this is supposed to be your day off—"

"We had to come see you," Tim said.

"Yeah," Jim said. "Came to apologize."

"Apologize?" Frank asked, sitting down on the railing so that his back was to the strong sun. It felt good.

"It's part of our bargain."

"Yeah. We have to be cooperative, for a whole week."

"Miss Rebecca explained to us why you couldn't afford to pay us as much as you were, and how it was better for you to put some of the money in the bank for us," Tim said, evidently trying to be very grown-up and unemotional.

"She explained compound interest and credit ratings, too," Jim added.

"From now on, you just put it all in the bank for us," Tim said, and Jim nodded decisively. "Next summer we're going to set up our own lawn business."

"What'll I do then?" Frank asked.

"Find some other kids who need the work," Tim said, as though Frank should have known that all along.

"Miss Rebecca is really neat, huh?" Jim asked seriously.

"Yeah, neat!" Tim agreed. "Don't you think so, Frank?"

Frank nodded. "Look, guys, I think we'll take a little time off until Tuesday. I've got other things to do."

"Church stuff?" Jim asked.

"Yes," Frank said with a sigh. "And I was pushing myself a little too hard. I didn't realize it until last night."

"Hey, we understand," Tim said, brightening. "Does Miss Ruth need anything done? We have to hang around until Mrs. Hobbs gets back, 'cause the bikes are still in her car."

"It might be a good time to weed her vegetables," Frank said. It was a job they'd argued with him about.

"Okay," Jim said, willing to make a sacrifice.

"Miss Ruth! We're going to weed your vegetables!" Tim called through the screen door.

"All right, boys," Ruth called back. "I'll make some lemonade for you."

Frank smiled after them as they scrambled off the porch and raced out to the shed where the truck was parked. Yes, he had to agree that Miss Rebecca must indeed be neat, if she could light such a spark in the Blakesley twins. The spark she'd ignited in him, however, was a different thing entirely.

Maybe, in their naiveté, the boys hadn't recognized the jealousy that had soured the air the afternoon they'd all been working in the garage and Rebecca had shown up. He'd wanted the opportunity to talk with her by himself, but the boys had been there, and suddenly it had seemed as though she were *their* buddy, not his. It was funny now that everything had worked out.

It hadn't been just that the boys were angry with their father and with him. They were beginning to sense what manhood was about, and they were confused. They probably didn't even discuss that between themselves; maybe they never would. It was just a part of growing up.

Frank left the porch and went back to writing his sermon.

Chapter Eight

Rebecca almost flew into the kitchen, her legal pad under her arm. "Mama! I have the greatest news!"

"Yes, dear, I know," Margaret said without much interest as she filled the teakettle. "Thelma told me she's bringing the board of the restoration society over here to discuss your signing Mrs. Gruber's house over to them."

"I just can't ever surprise you, can I?" Rebecca asked, opening the refrigerator to get some iced tea.

"Well, I certainly didn't expect to have to entertain this afternoon," Margaret said, as near to a snit as Rebecca had ever seen her.

"Mama, it's about the only way this is going to get worked out," Rebecca said. "I want to take care of as much as I can before I go back to Atlanta. Besides, your hair looks nice and you never have a bit of trouble coming up with a little tea and cookies. I'll even get the cookies over at the bakery."

"Oh, well, the ladies will realize it's a spur-of-the-moment thing, won't they?" Margaret asked. "Normally I wouldn't even think of getting cookies at the bakery."

"Are you still worried about Daddy, Mama?" Rebecca asked.

Margaret restrained herself from running her hand through her newly coiffed hair. "Yes, dear. I just know he's avoiding me!"

"Mama, you said yourself he's overworked. It's probably nothing a little fishing trip won't cure," Rebecca assured her. "Look at me! I was lower than a worm's belly when I got home Monday. Now I feel like taking on the world. Daddy's been working hard, and he probably just needs a vacation. What's the matter? You certainly can't think he's lost interest in you, can you?"

"Well, it's crossed my mind," Margaret admitted.

"No, you just forget that silliness," Rebecca said, hugging her mother, much as Margaret had hugged her when she'd come home earlier that week. "Oh! The boys' bikes are still in your car. I'd better get them out before you have to take the car out again. You know what I discovered, talking to them?"

"Hm?" Margaret asked, putting tea bags into a large plastic pitcher.

"Someone has made a lot of promises to them and not followed through," Rebecca said. "That's one thing I never had to worry about. If you made a promise and I kept my part of a bargain, you always came through. Or at least you tried."

"Well, I'm glad I did something right," Margaret said, smiling uncertainly. "Leave the bikes in the back of my car. I just won't use it until the boys come by. They should have to get the bikes out themselves."

"All right," Rebecca said, seeing her mother's brand of justice in the idea. "Look, I'll run over to the bakery. Do you need anything else?"

"Maybe some sandwich bread, dear," Margaret said, her old self again. "And stop by the deli for some sandwich fillings. Two small ones—maybe cream cheese. You decide what looks good to you."

Oh, if Big Ted got the appointment to the federal judgeship, Margaret was going to be surprised. But how was it going to work out if he didn't get it? Rebecca worried. Would he be able to mend his fences?

Rebecca expected a late-arriving member of the restoration society to be at the door when the bell rang, but the Blakesley boys were there, obviously having worked somewhere that morning, from the look of their once-white T-shirts.

"We came for our bikes," Tim said.

"Wait a moment while I find the keys to Mama's car," Rebecca said in a hushed voice, trying to keep part of her attention on the discussion in the parlor.

" . . . whether she can keep the house up at all," someone was saying. "Why, the yard is a mess. . . ."

Tim Blakesley edged closer to the parlor door, a sly, attentive look in his eyes. He motioned to Jim to follow him.

" . . . take a lot of work to make the place presentable . . ."

" . . . But to convince the tax collector's office to recognize the property as a potential museum and reduce the taxes . . ."

Tim motioned for Rebecca to listen and whispered, "We'll give you tomorrow at Mrs. Gruber's for what you did for us today."

"What did I do for you guys?" Rebecca asked.

"We'll tell you later," Tim said. "Six hours, mowing and pruning, weeding if we can get around to it. Deal?"

"Deal," Rebecca said, shaking the hand he extended to her and going into the parlor. "Ladies, I just got two volunteers to do some yard work over at Mrs. Gruber's tomorrow. You know, if we showed some initiative in making the place look as nice as possible immediately, the tax collector would take the house's museum status more seriously."

Thelma pounded her gavel on the table in front of her. She soon had the women promising their own Saturday mornings and volunteering their husbands and assorted live-at-home children for a work party at Mrs. Gruber's house the next day. It took a little verbal arm-twisting, but no one seemed to mind sacrificing a shopping expedition or a round of golf. Lists were made and assignments were doled out as Tim and Jim stood just inside the door, smiling at some secret they shared.

"What are you guys getting out of this?" Rebecca asked, walking the boys out to the garage while Margaret served the refreshments.

"Customers," Tim said.

"What?" Rebecca asked, bewildered.

"Next year we're going into business for ourselves," Tim said.

"Lawns," Jim explained. "Those ladies have *big* lawns."

"In fact, we might start our business after we start school and we see how much time we have," Tim said. "Maybe raking leaves and helping people get ready for winter."

Rebecca paused before unlocking the back of the station wagon and stared at them. "I didn't intend for you guys to—"

Jim interrupted her. "But you explained everything to us."

"So we decided, why work for somebody else?" Tim said.

"Indeed!" Rebecca said, moving aside as Tim started to open the back of the station wagon.

"Eight o'clock tomorrow," Tim said, taking a bike from the car. "We'll get an early start before it gets too hot."

"Good idea," Rebecca said.

"Thanks, Miss Rebecca," Jim said, mounting one of the bicycles and taking a turn around the pavement in front of the garage.

"Yeah, you've been a big help. We'll see you tomorrow!" Tim said, hopping on his bicycle and heading down the drive, followed quickly by Jim.

"I think I've created a monster!" Rebecca said with a laugh as she slammed the back of the station wagon closed and started back into the house. With that problem solved, all she had to do was meet their parents that afternoon.

Rebecca tied into her breakfast the next morning with gusto, knowing that she had a long day ahead of her working on Agnes Gruber's lawn. She'd dropped by the day before to explain to her just what would be happening and warn her that she might rather go visit someone while the lawn-mowing and cleaning up were going on, but Agnes had seemed thrilled at the idea of people being around. She was even happier to know that she could stay in her house as long as she wanted and that someone else would be responsible for the upkeep.

Now, sipping her orange juice, Rebecca smiled to herself, pleased that things were turning out so well. She had a few legal loose ends to tie up, but they would have to wait until later. Today she was just going to enjoy helping a neighbor and catching up on the town gossip at the same time.

Big Ted came in from his morning exercise, wiping his forehead with a handkerchief he carried in the back pocket of his running pants. "Morning, darling," he said. "It's going to be a hot one for your chores today!"

"Not to worry," Rebecca said. "Many hands make light the work. If they all show up!"

"I saw the boys pushing mowers in that direction," Big Ted said, searching the cupboard for a glass for his juice. "Mama isn't up yet?"

"Nope."

"She just turned over and went back to sleep," Ted said. "Not like her at all."

"Daddy, she's getting kind of upset with you," Rebecca said teasingly, preparing to rinse her dishes and put them in the dishwasher. "She thinks you don't love her anymore."

"It's not easy on me, either," Big Ted said with a sigh. He lowered his voice. "This appointment is taking longer than I'd expected. Now I guess it's not coming at all. Well, I'll make it up to her. Maybe today. We'll do something special. Do you have a date for tonight?"

"Come on, Daddy! Who would I have a date with?"

Big Ted grinned. "Frank."

"You're kidding!"

"Oh, come on, Reba! Ministers are just people. They fall in love, get married, all that. Where do you think preachers' kids come from?"

"But, Dad! Me? This is the kid you had to flash the porch light on. This is the kid you had to give very explicit lectures to, I seem to recall. I'm certainly not preacher's-wife material."

"I think that's a matter you may have to take up with the preacher."

"He certainly doesn't think that way about me!"

Big Ted lowered himself into his customary chair. "Darling, I have a spare pair of bifocals in my study desk. I think you might need them. The man is definitely attracted to you. And I can't fault his taste!"

"Daddy, you're prejudiced!" Rebecca said with a laugh, bending down to kiss his cheek. "And I love you for it. But you're wrong. I have to get over to Mrs. Gruber's."

Just then the phone rang in the judge's study.

"Want me to get that?" Rebecca asked.

"No," Big Ted said, getting to his feet. "You run along."

"I never expected this much of a turnout for hard work," Rebecca marveled as she poured some tea into a foam cup and sat down on the wooden steps that led to the front porch of Agnes Gruber's house.

Thelma Pettigrew laughed and sat down beside her. "All it takes is a little gentle persuasion."

The lawn mowers had finally finished, and the boys were telling some other teenagers how to prune the overgrown crape myrtle and pyracantha bushes.

"I always thought this house would look nice in cream with brown trim," Thelma mused. "Wasn't it nice of Fred Clark to donate the paint?"

Rebecca wondered how much talking Fred's wife, Sandra, had had to do to get the hardware store owner to donate paint, glass and nails and the other supplies to make minor repairs. "Tax write-off," she mumbled.

"Ah-a! So that's what you're up to!"

"Oh, come on, Thelma, I didn't do this for a write-off!" Rebecca exclaimed. "It was just something I had to do for my hometown."

Somewhere in the yard, a kid turned up the portable radio he'd been listening to and yelled, "Listen to this!"

"... who has been a judge in Kerry County for nearly fifteen years, was named this morning to the federal bench in Atlanta, pending confirmation. Judge Hobbs is well-known for innovative sentencing of youthful offenders in the rural area."

Rebecca's jaw dropped. "He got it! He got it! Daddy's going to be a federal judge!" She was jumping up and down, not even caring that she'd spilled her iced tea on the faded jeans she was wearing.

"Well, now!" Thelma grinned. "That's wonderful. Maybe that's why Margaret's been so on edge lately—"

"She didn't know anything about it," Rebecca explained. "Daddy was keeping it from her so she wouldn't be disappointed if it didn't come through. Oh, he's worked so hard over the years. I'm so proud!"

"I'm sure we're all proud that one of our own people is so well thought of as to be named to the federal bench," Thelma said.

Rebecca didn't remind her that Big Ted was a transplant in Blakesley Hills and had felt like an outsider until he'd lived there for over ten years.

"It leaves an interesting opening in the county, hmmm?" Rebecca mused, smiling back at Thelma.

"That it does," Thelma said thoughtfully, then winked.

"I think I'll check on the women who are doing the inside windows and woodwork," Rebecca said, starting up the porch steps into the house.

"Well, there's the man of the hour right now," Thelma said, waving as Big Ted drove up to the curb with Margaret by his side.

Willing hands helped unload the picnic cooler from the back of the car while Big Ted received congratulations from housepainters and yard workers alike. A secret look passed between father and daughter before they hugged each other.

"I felt bad about not volunteering to work today," Margaret explained. "So I thought we'd bring some lunch."

"This is lovely," Thelma said as she directed some of the teenage girls to set things out on an old picnic table under the trees in the backyard.

Margaret took Rebecca aside. "Daddy says you knew about this," she said, "but he swore you to secrecy."

Rebecca shrugged. "We didn't want you to be disappointed if he didn't get the appointment."

"Why, shame on you for ever doubting Daddy would get it!"

Rebecca laughed. "I never doubted. Daddy still has a touch of humility, it seems."

Another station wagon drew up to the curb, and the Blakesley twins left the hedge they were pruning to saunter over to it. Wanda Blakesley got out and opened the back door so that they could lift out several cases of canned soda pop and three bags of ice. She was about to get back into the car when she stopped and looked back at one of the boys. Then she laughed and settled in the driver's seat.

Rebecca wondered what had been said, because Wanda's attitude had changed in those few seconds. Maybe the boys were changing more than just their attitude toward Frank and herself. That was what she was hoping for, anyway.

A familiar white truck pulled up to the curb just as Wanda drove away. Rebecca's heart caught in her throat as she watched Frank slide out and come around to the passenger side of the truck. She was drawn down the steps and across the yard to see what he was doing.

"Miss Ruth sent cookies and lemonade," he told her. He handed her a cake pan covered with aluminum foil and then hefted an oversize picnic jug from the floorboards.

"Mm, they're still warm. That's sweet of her," Rebecca said, "but not unexpected. Come see what we've been doing."

"I can hardly miss it!" Frank said with a laugh.

"Daddy and Mama just came by," she told him. "Did you hear the big news?"

"What big news?"

"I'll let Daddy tell you. Tim! Come take this jug so Frank can go talk to my father."

"Are we breaking for lunch?" Tim asked.

"We might as well get the food before the ants and flies do," Rebecca said warmly.

Jim came running over and wrestled the cookies from her so that she could follow Frank. Big Ted was receiving the greetings of the people who were working on the house, some of the most successful businessmen and professionals in the county.

"...so the old firm is getting together at the Kerry Knolls Country Club tonight to celebrate," Big Ted was saying. "Oh, Frank, you come along as our guest, too. We'll stop by about six for you and Ruth."

The Blakesley twins spirited Frank off to assess their yard work almost before he could accept Big Ted's invitation, but the invitation was accepted. Rebecca shook her head and sidled up to her father when the crowd around him flowed toward the picnic lunch in the backyard.

"I could have asked him along myself, Daddy," she said.

"You could have," Big Ted agreed, a twinkle in his eye. "But he would have felt uncomfortable about it. We wouldn't want that."

Margaret came along, on a beeline to the car, her mind clearly set on a dozen things she had to do before dinner tonight. "Becca, that white linen dress is still in your closet. I thought I'd see if it needs a little pressing."

"I told you to give that to a garage sale," Rebecca said.

"Oh, no, dear. That's a classic. You never let something like that out of your hands," Margaret scolded. "You don't have anything else with you, do you?"

"No." Rebecca knew when she was licked. "I just hope I can get myself presentable in time." She pointed out the grass stains on her jeans. The twins had decided she was best suited to weeding around shrubs, which was neither an easy nor neat chore.

"Well, don't stay all day," Margaret said, letting herself into the car. "Jobs like this are never really finished."

Rebecca agreed.

"Where did you guys get those lawn mowers?" Frank asked the boys, looking down at the equipment they'd been using.

"The barn at home," Tim said.

"We cleaned 'em up and got 'em to work," Jim said proudly.

Frank looked at them questioningly. "This is really great of you guys to volunteer to work at this, but why have you gone to so much trouble getting these old relics going?"

"We're going to start a business when school starts," Tim said. "We're going to do lawns and stuff like that. You can have your carpentry and fixin'-up work and we'll do lawns. We wouldn't be takin' any of your business."

"We'll make some money for college," Jim said.

"Besides," Tim said, lowering his voice slyly, "if we have a good business, Dad won't be so likely to send us away to school."

Frank scratched his chin thoughtfully. "I don't know about this, boys," he said.

Tim wiped his hands on his jeans and waved to a cute girl who was passing on the way to the picnic table. "Miss Re-

becca explained all about business. Hey, we'll be million-
aires by the time we're twenty! C'mon, let's eat!''

Rebecca was lucky to find a sandwich, some chips and a
couple of her Aunt Ruth's pecan cookies when she got to the
picnic table. Tim handed her a foam cup filled with lemonade, and she went to sprawl in the shade of a dogwood
tree to relax.

Frank wandered slowly in her direction, and she wondered if he was trying not to attract attention. The man just
didn't know how handsome he was, black hair thick and just
barely tamed, tanned skin glowing, black eyes flashing with
humor and pleasure and all the positives that influenced
him.

The fact that he was walking straight toward her now sent
a thrill through her. He was wearing a black tunic with a
white collar, his strong, tanned arms swinging below the
short sleeves. Light gray slacks moved easily to accent his
long legs.

No, he wasn't a man who could hide himself.

"I was wondering about tonight," he said before he
reached her. "I've never been to the country club. I suppose I should wear a suit and tie."

"Going incognito?" Rebecca asked.

"I thought it might be more comfortable for . . . the others."

"This time of year, no one wears a suit to the club," Rebecca said. "Just knit shirts and slacks, that sort of thing."

"Thanks," he said starting to turn away. "I thought I
ought to ask before I really messed up. I'd stay and talk, but
I'm on my way to visit someone in the Milledgeville hospital, and I'm already behind schedule."

Rebecca watched him leave, then sighed and threw what
was left of her sandwich down on the wrapper spread on the

grass beside her. So much for the half-born fantasy she'd concocted in those few moments of them sitting there in the shade, talking endlessly of existential philosophy. Of course, in her fantasy, she was wearing a white linen dress, not a sweaty T-shirt and grass-stained jeans.

Chapter Nine

Frank didn't know when he had been so nervous. His ordination, probably. He had another chance to see Rebecca, and he hoped nothing went wrong this time. He hadn't exactly put the Blakesley twins out of his mind, but they shouldn't actively cause any trouble tonight.

His problem was that he was falling in love with a beautiful woman who was probably leaving to go back to Atlanta tomorrow, and he would see very little of her after that—unless he did something about it tonight.

He glanced into the streaked mirror over the painted dresser. His hair was a little longer than he would have liked it to be. Another white hair. He plucked it out and dropped it in the wastebasket by his desk.

Time to make some big decisions, a little voice told him. *Time waits for no man.*

"Frank? Big Ted and Margaret are coming," Miss Ruth called up to him. "Are you ready?"

"I'll be right there," Frank said, taking his wallet, jack-knife and a fresh handkerchief from the embroidered linen doily on top of the dresser and cramming them into the proper pockets of his light gray slacks.

Ruth was waiting for him at the bottom of the steps in her best summer dress, ready to let Margaret and Big Ted in.

"You look very nice," she said, in a tone she'd probably reserved for her boys when they'd taken extra pains to be presentable.

"I'm not really comfortable not wearing my collar out in public," he told her, running his hand along the back of his waist to check that his black knit shirt was tucked into his slacks.

"Now don't be silly," Ruth said, pushing the screen door open so that Margaret could enter. "He's afraid he doesn't look nice, sis. Tell him he looks fine."

"Yes, you certainly do, Frank," Margaret said.

"Where's Rebecca?" Ruth asked, voicing the question that had run through Frank like a flash of lightning.

"Well, she needed a little longer to get ready than we did," Big Ted said, coming into the house. "She'll meet us over at the club. Come on, I thought we'd drive by Mrs. Gruber's so you could see how all the work turned out."

It amused Frank that Margaret insisted he ride in the front seat of the sedan with the judge. Big Ted drove slowly through the streets and pulled up at the curb in front of Mrs. Gruber's house.

The fresh coat of paint, the extensive trimming and pruning of the lawn and the fresh plantings around the porches added immense charm to the old house.

"I never would have believed it," Ruth exclaimed. "Well, now we know what neighbors can do for someone in this town."

"It just takes someone to organize it," Margaret said as the car rolled away from the curb. "Agnes Gruber gave Rebecca the loveliest old crocheted tablecloth to pay her for her legal work. Rebecca was still stunned when she showed it to me. There's not a knot to be seen, front or back."

Frank felt his insides tighten when they drove through the entrance of the Kerry Knolls Country Club and he saw the lawn sprinklers spraying long plumes of water over the greens and fairways. He was reminded of the people he'd worked with for three years. They'd had to drill a well to replace one lost in an earthquake. Each drop of water had been precious; here it seemed squandered.

"Do you play golf?" Big Ted asked him.

"No," Frank said.

"Tennis?"

"A little," Frank confessed. "It's been a long time, though."

"I'll make arrangements for you to use the courts when you want them," Big Ted offered.

"That's nice of you, but I don't have the time."

"Nonsense," Big Ted said. "You've got to unwind sometime. Why do you think I run every morning? It's to get all the aggressions out."

Frank chuckled. "I don't allow myself aggressions."

Big Ted pulled up under the club's marquee and slipped the car into park. "I didn't know one had a choice in the matter," he said with a laugh. Then he got out of the car and handed it over to a valet.

Frank followed them into the club and eventually to the patio that adjoined a magnificent pool, beyond which lay several tennis courts and the first tee of the golf course. He stared at it all, taking everything in, then turned back to the people Big Ted wanted to introduce him to. He paid attention to the names and occupations and professions; he was trained to make these connections, because they were important if he was to be effective in the community. But this was a part of his calling that made him uncomfortable.

He was exchanging small talk with a man who suddenly looked past him and smiled. Following his line of vision, Frank saw Rebecca picking her way along the patio, politely greeting everyone, unhurried and cheerful. Her white linen dress was in startling contrast to the stained jeans and T-shirt he'd last seen her wearing.

But no matter what she wore, she always moved with an elegance and grace he found heart-stoppingly attractive. Rebecca was as sparkling and vivacious as he'd ever seen her, and perhaps more. As she bent slightly to listen to Miss Ruth, her hand rested on her aunt's shoulder with a telling familiarity.

"Oh, my, I was just a catalyst, Aunt Ruth!" he heard her say. "Catalyst? Well, that's just someone who puts things together, then stands back and watches them work."

Big Ted was in his glory, shaking hands with all the brotherhood of lawyers who'd shown up for the impromptu celebration. "Oh, you're just glad to see me go," he said to one of the men, who was known to disagree with His Honor over a ruling now and again.

"He wants to run for your seat," someone else gibed.

Rebecca laughed at the lawyers' banter and winked at Thelma Pettigrew, who was hovering by her husband. It might be an interesting race, she thought, but her money was on Thelma getting Carl elected to the county bench. Well, it made sense.

She turned away, thinking Frank Andrews would be nearby. Instead, Walter Minnifield, one of her father's old partners, broke from the group and began to stroll along the patio with her, signaling to the other partner to follow.

"Well, you surely put a crimp in ERM Properties, young lady," he said.

Rebecca raised an eyebrow. "I didn't do it to thwart them as much as to help Mrs. Gruber."

He shrugged. "Call it what you will, it was clever and very civic-minded. You're a chip off your old dad!"

"We never could keep him from taking on *pro bono* work, or cases where we knew he'd never see a cent of his fee. It was a boost to our revenues when he was elected to the bench," Edwin Drake joked.

"When I was a kid and I was thinking about studying law, I intended to be just like him," Rebecca confessed. "I guess I'd gotten sidetracked into corporate law."

Walt Minnifield lowered his voice. "We've heard that you're perhaps looking for a new position," he said. "We're prepared to offer you a junior partnership for two years, with an option to become a full partner."

"Oh, come on," Rebecca said in disbelief. "Just because of Daddy—"

"No! Listen! I've got one client who pays a good retainer who would love to be represented by a woman. We need someone to take small cases. Really, Rebecca, this is a *serious* offer."

"I have my ties to Atlanta. I know what's going on there. I'd have to think it over," she said, putting them off politely.

"Call the office when you're ready to talk and we'll arrange a time," Ed Drake said. "It's not an offer that we're going to withdraw quickly."

Rebecca smiled, dismissing their offer as a gesture. Lawyers seldom did anything quickly, she thought to herself.

There was a buzz around the patio as a waiter announced that a large table had been arranged for the party. Rebecca held back for a moment, acknowledging to herself that she was surprised and stunned to have been offered a position with her father's old firm. She was reminded of the joke about the stationery not having been changed. It was as though her homecoming were predestined. But she didn't believe in things like that, of course.

She felt a pressure at her elbow and looked up to see Frank beside her. "Good evening, Rebecca," he said.

"Well, Reverend Andrews," she said formally, looking up at him with a bright smile. "Blending in with the surroundings. I see you took my advice."

"Yes," he said, and was surprised that that much came out. He was fairly dazzled by the way Rebecca looked, by the way the scent of jasmine wafted around her in the warm evening air. She was a constant puzzle to him, like a many-sided crystal, beautiful from every aspect, but always different.

He wasn't paying much attention to anything but her when the crowd on the patio began to move and she slipped her hand into the crook of his arm.

Rebecca hadn't meant to be preoccupied over dinner. She enjoyed sitting beside Frank, having diplomatically taken a seat at the far end of the table to allow her parents' friends to be closer to them, knowing she had more time to enjoy their company than their friends did.

Frank looked devastatingly handsome—as usual. Rebecca sensed that he was enjoying this opportunity to step back from his vocation and the attention it focused on him. He'd seemed to let out a breath he'd been holding when Big Ted had asked another lawyer to recite a prayer for lawyers and judges as the grace before the meal.

Most of the people at the table were old friends of the Hobbs family, and Rebecca was drawn into their conversations and their jokes, but she felt uneasy about the annoyance she sensed coming from Frank.

Frank sat quietly, also, as though he were studying his surroundings and the people at the table he hadn't met before. His attitude made Rebecca self-conscious, as though he, too, were carefully weighing everything she did and said and she might be found wanting.

She wasn't surprised that he took the first opportunity after the meal to push his chair back. "I think I'll get some air," he said, rising to his feet.

"Mind if I come with you?" Rebecca asked. "I'd hate for you to get lost in a sand trap."

A sunset was dying over the magnificent old oaks as Rebecca and Frank strolled to the far end of the patio. Rebecca thought that she might not be out-of-bounds if she reached out and touched his arm to feel the warmth and strength that was coiled there. But she hesitated.

"You did a good job with Mrs. Gruber's house," he said.

Rebecca could tell from his tone that he was just making polite conversation, and she laughed, politely. "Thirty-seven people had a hand in working on Mrs. Gruber's house," she told him. "I spent most of my time pulling weeds and cheering everyone else on. Tim and Jim did the mowing and supervised the lawn work. I was very proud of them. You've trained them well."

Frank crossed his arms in front of him and rocked back on his heels. It was a posture Rebecca recognized as something men did when they had a load of anger and didn't want any of it to get out. In the dim light she could see the tense line of his jaw harden.

"They were telling me about a little business they plan to start this fall, thanks to your lecture Friday morning," he said, his tone becoming accusatory. "I thought it was cute when they came over to apologize to me for being angry, but now they've turned into junior entrepreneurs.''

"What's so bad about that?" Rebecca asked.

"In one day you undid everything I tried to accomplish with them in teaching them ethics and morals," Frank muttered.

"Now just a minute!" Rebecca countered. "First of all, there's nothing immoral or unethical about running a business to make a profit. We've been over that before. I merely showed the boys why you had to change your way of paying them. They seemed interested in the concepts I was explaining, so we went into it pretty deeply.''

"So now they've got dollar signs in their eyes."

"Frank, that's not my fault," she protested. "Naive young boys often go through that phase. I remember it with my brother Don. At least now they're thinking of something other than being miserable and wanting to run away without being caught.''

Frank unfolded his arms and shoved his hands into his back pockets. "I still don't like it. I worked very hard with those boys. I tried not to be pushy, tried the intellectual approach. I didn't foist my values on them. And you ruined everything.''

"Okay! Have it your way! *I* ruined everything. There might be a time when they remember something you've told them and it will make a difference. Nothing you teach the boys will ever be lost or forgotten. But let them explore this new idea until they've put it into perspective with everything else in their minds. You may find out that they have a talent for making money.''

"Money, money, money! That's all people think about?" Frank exploded. "Those people at the table tonight, talking about their real estate deals and their investments." He turned away from her and stared out at the lawn. "If you had seen the way people were living in the last place I worked—''

Rebecca put her hand on his shoulder. ''I understand that it was a desperate situation, that everything had to be rebuilt after an earthquake. But you're *here* now, Frank. It would be nice for those people to have what we do, but it's impossible. I've lived in Atlanta for a while, and even though I have a nice place and make good money I've realized I can't do an awful lot about poverty, even though I had great dreams about righting all the world's wrongs when I was a kid.''

''Well, the worst of what you see in Atlanta would probably be welcomed in—'' Frank's voice faltered.

''No, it wouldn't,'' she said firmly. ''Poverty is poverty, and it's not pretty. Obviously some power decided you'd done what you could do with the situation you were in and sent you here to help this place. You're a lot like Tim and Jim, holding on to something else when a new opportunity opens up. We've been trying to get them to accept the present, and both of us have been holding on to the past.''

She laughed at the irony of it all. ''Except, being here this week, I've almost completely forgotten why I came home in the first place. I was intending to be in London tonight, going to the theater and hearing Big Ben mark the hours. Then a friend suggested that I needed to come home. Do you believe in greater plans? *I* do. If I hadn't come home, Mrs. Gruber's house might belong to ERM Properties right now, and the Blakesley twins might be putting another coat of paint on their great-great-grandfather.''

Frank laughed in spite of himself. ''A greater plan? Yes, I guess I have to believe in that.''

''Then you're here because, for now, this is where you're supposed to be,'' Rebecca said.

''But I can't forget about the other place....''

Rebecca shrugged. "Then don't. But there's no reason to suffer for it or to make us suffer because we're not poor enough to make you feel like a great man for helping us out."

"Oh, you think my ego is involved?" Frank asked.

Rebecca, sensing she'd gone too far, backed away. "Sorry."

Frank turned and stared at her for a long moment, and Rebecca sensed that a battle was going on within him. His dark gaze flashed at her, then went dull and skittered away toward the lawns beyond the patio. "The truth is, my ego is *too* involved," he admitted with difficulty. "That's one of the faults I have to overcome."

"At least you recognize your failings. Believe me, there are men with much worse faults who think they're perfect. I think *that's* your true strength."

Frank looked at her as though he neither understood nor believed her, and she thought at that moment how very vulnerable he was, and how very magnetic. He turned away and looked out at the night gathering on the broad lawns.

"Frank," Rebecca said, and when he looked back at her she merely shook her head. "Look, I brought my own car. I'm tired from all the work I've done this week. I think I'll leave now. Want me to give you a ride home?"

"Yes, that sounds like a good idea."

When Rebecca drew up to the curb beside Ruth's house a short time later, the silence between them was almost a tangible object sitting somewhere in the vicinity of the shift console.

Frank shook his head in the darkness. "Something got out of sync Thursday night, and nothing has been quite right since then, has it?"

Rebecca laughed nervously. "Yes, I think that's where it took a wrong turn. What could we have done differently, though? We had to . . . find the boys."

"Well, *my* plans got scuttled by the rain," Frank said, sighing as he shifted his long legs in the cramped space in front of him. "If the weather hadn't been so bad, I was thinking of asking you to walk over to the Crispy Cone for an ice cream."

Rebecca stared at him for a long moment, then turned the key in the ignition and switched on the headlights. "Come on, then," she said.

"What? Where?" Frank asked as she steered out into the street.

"I'm giving us a second chance," she told him.

"But I—I left all but five dollars with the woman I went to see in the hospital today," he said with a groan. "And I need that for gas on Monday."

Rebecca laughed. "You put a lot of faith in the Lord to provide, don't you?"

"Well, yes," Frank said firmly.

"*My* treat," Rebecca said, sweeping away any objections he might have.

At the Crispy Cone, she pulled around to the drive-up window and fished her wallet out of her purse. "What do you want?" she asked, consulting the menu and her change purse.

"Really, after that dinner we had . . ." Frank shook his head. By now Rebecca knew there was no use trying to budge him. *A stubborn man. Just what I deserve.*

A barely intelligible voice asked for her order on the speaker. "A root-beer float," Rebecca said, forming the words distinctly. "Two straws."

Frank threw back his head and laughed, then wiped his eyes with the back of his hand. "You're something else."

When Rebecca got the float, she handed it, along with the paper napkins and the straws, to Frank and eased the car out into the street and turned toward the depot at Old Kerry. "These things always taste better under a big tree along a dirt road."

"At least I don't have to worry about us getting lost," Frank remarked, putting one straw on the dashboard. He handed the container back to her when she'd found a suitable setting.

"All right," Rebecca said, stripping the paper off her straw. "What now?"

Frank again refused the drink she offered him. "This is the hard part, isn't it? It's always awkward."

"Hey, you seemed to be doing all right this afternoon when you kissed me!" Rebecca teased.

"What? Oh, yes, back to Thursday night, huh? Well, that wasn't—"

"Oh, I thought it was!" Rebecca skimmed some of the froth from the top of the cup with the straw and then licked it off with her tongue—it was the only way to truly appreciate a root-beer float.

"Was what?"

"Whatever you wanted it to be," Rebecca said, digging the long-handled spoon into the thick foam on the top of the cup.

"I think I will have a taste of that ice cream," Frank said, turning and putting his hand on the back of her seat.

"Oh! Here..." Rebecca said, prodding the ice cream with the spoon.

"No, not like that," he said, placing his finger under her chin and raising it slightly. "You left a little bit right here...."

He kissed the corner of her mouth slowly. "Delicious."

"My, my, my..." Rebecca said a moment later. "You *are* a man of surprises."

"Would it surprise you to know that I've known a few back roads in my day?" he asked. "Although I can't recall that I ever did any nocturnal whittling or exterior decorating."

"I admire your restraint," Rebecca said, scooping a spoonful of ice cream out for him.

"I probably just didn't meet the right girl," he said with a shrug. Then he leaned back in his seat to savor the ice cream—or perhaps the moment.

"Would you believe that I never actively encouraged any of those . . . expressions?" she asked.

"I never thought you had to. I know *I* didn't need much of a push the first time I saw you. I got to thinking back the other night, and I can't believe it was so long since I was a kid like the boys. I forgot how like them I was. How I felt ignored. So I acted like a real dunce until I thought of a great way to get back at my father for his lack of attention."

Rebecca detected a note of devilishness in his voice. "Oh? What did you do?"

"I found I could make Father's life most miserable by espousing one of his causes and taking it to the extreme. It worked like a charm." Frank's voice became distant in the darkness. "I never thought it would lead to being taken over by the 'Big Boss.' I fought the call to the ministry harder than I fought doing what my earthly father wanted. I was severely overmatched. It seems I always am."

"I find that hard to believe," Rebecca said.

Frank chuckled. "Look, my arm is going to sleep behind your seat. Do you mind if I move it?"

"Of course not," she said, leaning forward and handing the float to him when he'd rearranged himself. "Here, hold this. We ought to go somewhere else. It's getting warm, and I don't like to run the air-conditioning when we're just sitting here." She turned the key in the ignition and switched the headlights on.

"Where did you have in mind?" he asked.

"The pond..." Rebecca backed out into the road, and a spray of gravel hit the underside of the car.

"Oh," Frank said flatly.

"Do you want to go somewhere else?"

"The back porch at your place?"

He cleared his throat and reached for the straw that had been lying on the dashboard. Rebecca watched him out of the corner of her eye as he unwrapped the second straw and pushed it into the container, then took a long swallow.

"Tsk, tsk! So much for resisting temptation," she said.

"There are temptations and there are temptations!" he said. "I do pretty well on the bad ones."

"Relax. I won't tell the bishop." she assured him.

There was a moment of silence, and then he laughed. It was a deep, rich sound that filled the night. "That's very funny," he said at last.

"I'm glad you appreciate my comedic talent," Rebecca said. She was slightly confused by his reaction. "You don't mind if I tease you about your calling?"

"No," he said, then chuckled. "There are lawyer jokes, too, you know."

She parked the car in the turnaround at the house and they walked slowly to the back porch, passing the float between them until it was finished.

The air was heavy with the scent of the trailing geraniums that hung in baskets on the porch, and the crickets competed with the muffled sounds of someone having a cookout in the next block.

They sat on the porch swing, pushing it gently forward and backward and enjoying its comfortable creaking noise. Frank tilted his head and studied Rebecca's face in the dim light.

"You are a temptation, Miss Rebecca," Frank said. "A very big temptation."

Rebecca stared back at him, at a loss for words. "I assure you I have no intention of luring you from the straight and narrow," she said when she found her voice at last.

"I never thought for a moment that you did. It's just that for the past six years of my life I've steered clear of female distractions, and just when I'm at my worst you show up!"

"What do you mean, at your worst?" Rebecca asked teasingly. "You look quite respectable to me."

The porch swing glided forward and backward a couple times before Frank seemed ready to speak.

"You know the saying about it always being darkest before the dawn?" he asked. "Well, for me it's about five minutes to six. It might not look like it to you at the moment, but I've just about gotten my life together. Rebecca, no matter how much hell-raising I did as a kid, I always had certain standards I lived by, in my heart. Regarding women, especially. For me, it's marriage or nothing. It's not only a matter of setting a good example for my congregation or avoiding embarrassment or scandal. It's a matter of a commitment to myself and to whoever I'll marry not to have a lot of excess baggage in the relationship."

"And my reputation is unacceptable excess baggage?" Rebecca asked.

"Oh, no! Don't jump to that conclusion. I didn't mean that at all."

"Then what did you mean?"

"That if we become close friends, and the more time I spend with you the more I strongly believe that's unavoidable, there's only one logical outcome, and that's marriage, an old-fashioned, long-lasting, faithful marriage. So I'm warning you now that *that's* the type of relationship I see for myself, so you can run the other way now, before our lives get too entangled.''

''I hope you're not intending that to be a marriage proposal, because it sounds more like a business contract.''

''Believe me, if and when I propose marriage, you'll know exactly what my intentions are! But I wanted to tell you what my personal ground rules are, to leave you an out. With...with your father's new position, your life might have some twists and turns in it that will put an end to—''

''I don't see why,'' Rebecca told him. ''Daddy's new position has nothing to do with me. At least I don't think so.''

''I hope not,'' Frank said with a sigh, stretching his arm along the back of the swing. ''I might as well resign myself to the fact that nothing ever works out easily in my life. I find the most beautiful, intelligent, clever, witty woman I've ever known, and she lives an hour's drive away.''

''That's not so far....''

''You haven't ridden in my truck,'' Frank said warmly, ruffling his hand through Rebecca's short brown hair. ''As you so correctly pointed out, I take myself too seriously at times, aside from having a temper and a healthy dose of impatience when the world doesn't go my way. Overcoming those shortcomings will be a lifetime project. I think it will probably take someone with a sense of humor and the audacity to make me face myself to cope with me. I see those qualities in you.''

''I think you're reading too much into a little moonlight and a root-beer float, Frank. I'm not used to getting terribly serious about a man after knowing him only a few days,'' she told him. ''Even though...''

''Even though what?'' he asked, moving closer to her.

"I've never felt as much honesty as I feel with you."

Frank looked at her seriously for a moment. "I've been as honest with you as I can be, but . . . well, there are things that are better left buried in the past and around the edges."

"Around the edges?" Rebecca said with a laugh. "Are you hiding something from me, Frank?"

He shook his head. "Not as much hiding something as just not making an issue of it."

Rebecca laughed. "I knew it! Dark-haired men *are* dangerous and secretive—even when they're supposed to be angels."

"I'm no angel," Frank said. He proved it by kissing her. It was a slow, passionate kiss that left no question about the affection that was growing between them. For the first time Rebecca felt free to respond to him, to let herself trust him and show him the happiness she felt at their having found each other.

Rebecca wrapped her arms around him, reveling in the strength and security of their budding affection. This was a love she'd despaired of finding in men more concerned with themselves and their fortunes than in the world around them.

Their world was very small and very exclusive at the moment. The past was forgotten, and the future was far away. Only this moment mattered.

"How long have we known each other?" Frank asked when Rebecca rested her head on his shoulder and sighed.

"Forever," she answered.

Chapter Ten

Frank determinedly read his sermon from the dog-eared pages he'd written it on. Every time he looked at the congregation his eyes were drawn to Rebecca. She sat between her parents, stylish and cool in a light sundress and a broad-brimmed straw hat. If he looked at her too long he would lose his place, so he followed his script closely, marking his place with his thumb.

It seemed like the longest service he'd ever conducted, although the pocket watch he'd placed on the podium reminded him he was right on schedule. His chasuble was itching around his shoulders, and his collar seemed tighter than usual.

When it came time for the final hymn, he followed the recession of the choir to the rear of the church, where he pronounced the benediction. He wanted to bolt out of the vestibule and return to his cubbyhole office behind the sanctuary, where he could remove his heavy vestments. But as he shook hands with the parishioners he put that unworthy thought away from him.

The most popular topic of conversation that morning was Big Ted's appointment to the federal bench. Big Ted was the senior warden, the person appointed by the priest to advise him on parish business, and Frank had come to rely on Big Ted more than he'd realized. Margaret, as the head of every fund-raising endeavor, was being greeted with moans about the void she would leave in the church activities.

Frank shook Miss Ruth's hand, then Margaret's, and expected Rebecca to be next in line, but in the middle of talking to Margaret, he realized that Rebecca was nowhere to be seen. He shook Big Ted's hand. "We'll be over Tuesday morning to finish your garage," he said. "I have a commitment tomorrow."

"That's fine," Big Ted told him. "Since everything is closed in, there's no big rush."

"The way it rained this past week," Frank said, "we'll be doing lawns until we drop the rest of the week."

Wanda Blakesley was next in line. She was smiling, and she seemed less tense than Frank had ever seen her.

He said the first thing that came to mind. "Your boys did a fine job yesterday at Mrs. Gruber's."

"All we hear about now is their little business," Wanda said. "At least they're being positive."

"We spent all Friday evening working on those two old mowers," the colonel said, shaking his head. "I never knew Jim was so mechanically inclined."

"They're both constantly amazing me," Frank said warmly.

"Are you sure you don't need the boys tomorrow?" the colonel asked.

"I have to be out of town," Frank told him.

"Good. I think we'll grab the poles and take a little drive in the direction of some fish, maybe stay overnight," the colonel said, putting his arm around his wife.

"I'm sure the boys will enjoy that." Frank felt himself swell up a little. Someone had finally made the point with the colonel that he had to do something with the boys, not just talk about it. But he had a feeling there had been a little help from the conspicuously missing woman along the way.

It was the coward's way out to slip out the side door of the church, but kids had been doing that for as long as she could remember. Rebecca's conscience hardly felt a twinge. She told herself she was going that way to keep an eye on the Blakesley twins.

Two of the girls who'd worked at Mrs. Gruber's house the day before were waiting for the boys. They giggled and acted silly, but they finally got up their nerve to speak. The boys began to swagger a bit.

Rebecca shook her head, knowing how those encounters went, how little was said, and how crucial it seemed at the time. But she was glad the twins were being accepted in the community; that was the important thing.

Then she went about the chore she'd promised to do for her mother, taking the vase of flowers from the Sunday school room in the parish hall and wrapping them to be taken to one of the shut-ins that afternoon. Margaret had been besieged when the service had ended and had delegated Rebecca to handle the one problem in her morning.

Rebecca strolled slowly back to the parish hall and found the bouquet of multicolored gladioli, the contribution of someone's backyard garden. She carefully lifted the vase and carried it to the kitchen to drain the water from it.

Usually there was a stack of newspapers in the corner to wrap flowers with, but there was nothing. Nor were there any paper towels handy. Stymied, she stared at the flowers resting on the drainboard, then looked around the kitchen once more. There wasn't even anything to wipe her hands on!

Sighing, she left the kitchen and went down the hall to the ladies' room, dried her hands and grabbed a handful of rough brown paper towels to wrap the flowers in.

Coming out of the ladies' room, she nearly collided with Frank as he hurried to his office to remove his vestments. He'd already pulled the green brocade stole from around his neck and was folding it.

They both stopped dead in their tracks and stared at each other.

"Good morning," Frank said, his voice soft in the silence.

"Do you need any help with your vestments?" Rebecca asked. Reverend Higgins, his predecessor, had always had his wife to help him, especially with the heavy chasuble, the embroidered poncholike garment that slipped over his head.

"The boys are usually here to help me," Frank called back to her from inside his tiny office. "But they seem to have discovered girls, and their father wants to get them home so they can go fishing."

"Oh! Good for them. Just a minute—" She dashed into the kitchen, dumped the handful of towels on the drainboard, then returned to Frank's office.

Frank was placing his stole in a shallow drawer in the closet. When he turned to face her, his eyes held a troubled look.

"What's wrong?" Rebecca asked softly. "Is there some particular ritual to this that I don't know?"

"No, that's not it," he said. "I've just realized what it's going to mean to me for your parents to leave."

Rebecca shrugged. "We haven't discussed that much yet," she said, reaching out to help him lift the heavily embroidered chasuble over his head.

He held the chasuble while she slipped a thick wooden hanger under it, then hung it in the closet and covered it with a muslin dustcover.

"So this is what is meant by 'a man of the cloth,'" Rebecca quipped, smoothing the cover over the heavy garment.

"That's the hard part," he said, turning to her with a wry smile.

He expected her to leave, she thought, but she wasn't about to back away so easily.

While he untied the cincture, the heavy white rope belt that was tied around his waist, Rebecca reached for another hanger to receive the surplice, the simple white robe that covered him from shoulders to feet.

"I really can carry on from here," he told her as he placed the cincture with the stole and closed the drawer.

"No problem," Rebecca said. "All I have to do is wrap up some glads and take them to Mrs. Young."

He slipped out of the surplice and took the hanger from her hand. With his black slacks he wore a white T-shirt with a rabat, a black bib with a white collar attached. He sighed and flexed his shoulders.

"All that must be very uncomfortable on a hot day like today," Rebecca observed.

Frank nodded and reached for the jacket of his suit.

"But far be it from you to complain, right?" she asked.

"What good would it do?" He chuckled. "No, the vocation has its drawbacks. We just endure."

Frank settled his jacket on his shoulders, then pushed his hand through his hair and closed the door with a decisive shove. "Thank you."

"I—I have to take care of those flowers...." she said awkwardly.

But when she reached the kitchen Aunt Ruth was taking the flowers from the drainboard and wrapping them with the towels. "Your mother sent me to look for you," she said, barely looking up. Rebecca detected a certain humor in her attitude. "I'll run over to Mrs. Young's myself. She's going to sew some quilt patches for me."

"I'd better get going...." Rebecca said, inching toward the door.

"Your folks have already gone home," Aunt Ruth said.

"I can walk," Rebecca said.

Rebecca was aware of Frank coming into the kitchen and standing behind her. "Miss Ruth, will you lock that door on your way out? I'll check the sanctuary doors," he said.

"Always the last to leave." Ruth chuckled and hoisted the flowers. "Y'all have a nice afternoon."

Frank clasped Rebecca's hand and drew her along with him as he turned off lights and locked doors. The sanctuary held the scent of flowers and extinguished candles. The silence echoed with the lingering chords of the old pipe organ.

"Are you sure you have to go back to Atlanta?" Frank asked softly. He seemed to be in no hurry.

"I think I've done just about all the damage I can do around here," Rebecca said with a chuckle.

"The town will never be the same," Frank assured her.

"It hasn't changed much. So one of the oldest houses in town has a fresh coat of paint. So the town troublemakers are on their good behavior. So—"

"So the new minister is in worse shape than he was when he got here."

"Ah, Frank," Rebecca said with a sigh, all the doubts that had kept her awake the night before coming back to the forefront of her thoughts.

"It's nothing that can't be cured," he said, putting his arms around her waist and drawing her close to him.

"Frank!" Rebecca exclaimed. "Not here!"

Frank looked at her with a puzzled expression. "Why not?"

"It's the church!"

He laughed, then looked up at the vaulted ceiling and the stained-glass windows. "To me, this is home. I'm more comfortable here than anywhere else."

Rebecca tilted her head and studied his face. It was so innocent in this light. "I still feel as though we're trespassing," she told him. "Frank, I am not a church person. You would beg me not to sing in the choir. If I quote chapter and verse, it pertains to someone versus someone. The only thing I like about Sunday school is that there are no tests. Mama couldn't find a bribe big enough to get me to go to vacation bible school. Much as I feel something for you, I don't think this relationship has a future."

They were standing at the back of the church, near the double doors that led to the vestibule. Frank's face took on a serious expression. He was obviously thinking something through. Rebecca watched him fascinated, as his forehead creased above his straight black eyebrows.

"Do you honestly feel that way?" he asked, holding her hand to his chest.

Feeling his heart beating under the soft black fabric of his rabat, Rebecca nodded, then sighed. "Last night notwithstanding, I think it's best to step back from each other now, before we get too involved, before it hurts too much. Can you understand that?''

Frank smiled sadly and moved along to lock the heavy double doors to the street. At last they walked down the front steps of the church to the shady sidewalk.

"Come have dinner with us," Rebecca said, knowing her mother's roast beef and mashed potatoes would stretch to feed half a dozen people if it had to.

"No," Frank said softly. "I have work to do this afternoon."

"All right," Rebecca said.

It didn't solve anything, Rebecca thought as she walked along the sidewalk, avoiding the cracks in the uneven pavement, her feet already hurting in shoes not meant for walking.

She'd known Frank less than a week and she could barely remember what life had been like before she'd met him, but she knew she wasn't the kind of woman he needed.

She'd known from a fairly early age that she wanted to be a lawyer, and her parents had tactfully told her that to achieve that goal she would have to avoid the pitfalls other girls fell into. And she'd done that. But she'd also raised a few eyebrows in Blakesley Hills in her youth, and the citizens of the town, who tended to have long memories, wouldn't regard Rebecca and Frank as a match made in heaven.

No, there was no way this would work out. It was best to forget the whole thing.

Big Ted leaned back in his chair at the table on the back porch where they'd eaten their Sunday dinner and looked out at the yard. It was dappled with deep shade from the oak trees. "I've made one decision," he proclaimed.

"Shall I call a press conference?" Margaret asked, slightly light-headed from the whirlwind activities of the last day or so.

Big Ted laughed and reached out to take her hand. "We're not going to sell this house," he told her. "We've put too much into it. I think we'll just rent a place in Atlanta and come out here every chance we get. That way you needn't desert all the charity work you're doing here."

"I'd certainly like to desert some of it," Margaret said with a chuckle, spearing a bite of watermelon from her plate. "But I hate the thought of trying to find a place to live in Atlanta."

Rebecca sighed. "It will be good to have you in Atlanta," she said. "There are times when I need someone to talk to me who can give me advice I don't want to hear."

"Oh? Do you think I would do that?" Margaret asked.

"Yes, but only when I need it." She picked up her plate and started into the kitchen. "I think I'll go home this evening."

"You will?" Big Ted asked. "Aren't you leaving some unfinished business here?"

"Mrs. Gruber's house?" Rebecca asked. "I can come home and take care of that anytime."

"That's not what I mean, young lady," Big Ted said, following her into the kitchen, "and you know it."

"What do you mean?" Rebecca asked.

"Frank."

"What about him?"

"Well, I thought I saw definite indications of romantic fraternization there."

Rebecca took his plate and rinsed it with her own. "Daddy, if I knew what to do about Frank, I wouldn't be leaving."

Margaret came into the kitchen and edged her husband away from the sink. "Ted, don't you know there are some things young ladies want to talk over with their mamas, not their daddies?" she asked. "Now, you just go read your paper and watch your baseball game. Rebecca and I have some serious world problems to solve."

"Was I being so obvious?" Rebecca asked, loading the dishwasher.

"No, darling," Margaret said confidently, for the first time since Rebecca could remember closing the door that separated the kitchen from the back parlor. "Now, what makes you think that you should let that gorgeous man out of your grasp?"

"You mean you want me to—Mama, do you see me as the wife of a minister?"

"Well, now," Margaret said, settling into one of the chairs at the kitchen table, "about thirty years ago I went away to college thinking that I'd be a librarian, and I met a wonderful young law student while I was back in the stacks one day. At that time it didn't look like such a great prospect, but I saw sterling qualities in him. All the conventional guidelines no longer applied. And through all the hard times, through all the lean years, well, we just have had the best marriage I know of."

"And now it's paid off," Rebecca observed.

Margaret laughed. "No, my dear, it paid off long ago. With you and Donnie. The payment on an emotional investment, my child, isn't in dollars and cents, or even in success as the world sees it, but in happiness. I'm just hoping this new challenge doesn't overwhelm me. Entertaining for a federal judge is going to be much more difficult than it was at home here. I'm glad we're not giving up this place, though."

"I didn't come home looking for...a man," Rebecca said, leaning her elbows on the table.

"Well, one found you," Margaret said.

"I'm certain that Frank has other things on his mind, building up the parish and making a living—"

"Something tells me that you're very much on his mind."

"It's an awkward situation, Mama. How do you have a romance with someone whose life is under such scrutiny?"

"I've never seen you back away from the limelight before, Rebecca!" her mother said with a laugh. "You've never been shy about things like this."

"Well, I am now. I'm a lawyer, not a Sunday school superintendent or a missionary circle chairman. Mama, I have to be me, and he has to be himself, and I don't see it working out. I—I need to go back to Atlanta and check to see if I've gotten responses on any of my résumés."

"Something tells me you're calling this game before either of you gets up to bat. Becca, you're making a mistake."

"Mama, I'm not what he needs. I'm not innocent enough, charitable enough...patient enough."

"And you'd give up a man who is honest and kind and good, to say nothing of gorgeous and passionate, without even knowing how he feels about you? He deserves his day in court, dear."

"No, Mama, as soon as I get packed up, I'm going home to Atlanta," Rebecca said, getting to her feet slowly. "I've got a lot of things to do there."

Rebecca went into the laundry room and picked up the basket full of her clean clothes and took it up to her room. One thing that Rebecca was certain of was that once she made up her mind, right or wrong, she went through with it.

* * *

Rebecca cringed at the traffic of Atlanta as she drove toward her apartment. It wasn't like home, where everyone took his time. Atlanta seemed to have no such thing as a street without a bend or a hill in it.

Her mailbox was promisingly filled, but once she'd culled the junk mail and the bills there were only three hopeful responses to her résumés. She opened her briefcase to put them in and ran across the termination letter from George Halburton.

Kicking her shoes off, she sat down on her couch and read the letter, this time taking in every word, every nuance. And this time she got angry. Very angry.

"I'm surprised to see you back so soon," Jonathan Douglas said, looking up from his desk at Halburton Development the next morning. "Your vacation seems to have done you some good," he observed. "You've got a nice tan. I'm jealous."

"I was wondering when I could tell another firm I'm free of my obligations here," Rebecca told him. "Mr. Halburton isn't in yet."

Jonathan scratched his head and flipped through his desk calendar. "Almost immediately, I'd think. There's nothing pressing, is there? You cleared everything to take your vacation. Ballenger ought to be able to take over anytime."

Rebecca shrugged. She wished she could clear out her desk and leave today, rather than work with people she felt had stabbed her in the back.

"George is out of town this morning. I'm just about to call him about something that has come up."

"Go ahead," Rebecca said, turning away to sit down, not wanting him to see that she was gritting her teeth. "And let me have a word with him."

She waited patiently through greetings, idle chitchat and minor glitches. Then Jonathan handed the phone to her.

"George," she said, deciding to plunge right into the problem, "that letter you sent me must have had a typographical error in it. The severance pay is awfully low. I'm going to need, let's say, four months' salary to tide me over. Pickings appear pretty slim in the law job market."

George Halburton chuckled. "I suggest you take what you're offered and be satisfied with it."

"There are some government agencies that might like to hear about the fancy footwork you've done to get me to merge your company with another, and about how you dropped me in favor of the other firm's lawyer," she reminded him.

"How much did you say you wanted?" Halburton asked slowly.

"I'm not asking you for what I want," Rebecca said, having learned a few things about negotiating lately. "I'm telling you that I'll settle for four months' salary."

"All right," he said after a moment of thought.

Rebecca returned the phone to a stunned Jonathan.

"Any luck on your résumés?" Jonathan asked when he'd hung up the phone.

"Not much," Rebecca confessed. "But there were some ads in the Sunday paper I thought I'd check out today."

Jonathan pushed his chair back and drummed his fingers on the arm of his chair. "Look, anything that's advertised in the paper is probably the dregs. I'll give you the name of someone who can find you something worth your while."

He got out his briefcase and drew a business card from some secret recess. "Copy this down..."

* * *

The bishop's office was carpeted and furnished with Danish-modern desk and chairs. Frank had waited in the anteroom for fifteen minutes and was having a difficult time controlling his impatience.

His Eminence entered from another room and stretched out his hand in an automatic gesture. Then, looking into his face, he embraced Frank and patted him on the back.

"You're looking much better than you did three months ago, son," he said, letting go of him to sit down in his swivel chair. "How is everything going in Blakesley Hills?"

Frank settled into a chair and took all the facts and figures from the folder he was carrying. "We've increased the average attendance in church school by ten children each week, and the Sunday worship by seventeen. Considering that this is summer, I'm very encouraged."

"You don't look it," the bishop said with a dry laugh. "Frank, I sense another crisis here. Are you still upset about being brought back from the field, or are you doubting your calling again?"

"Neither," Frank said.

"Then what is it?" The bishop's dark eyes probed and would not go unanswered. "When you were younger I knew what that look meant."

"It means the same thing now, Father," Frank sighed. "Only this time I think it's fatal."

"What's her name?"

"Rebecca Hobbs."

"Big Ted Hobbs's daughter?" the bishop asked, obviously somewhat surprised. "Hmmm. I heard that Big Ted was named to the federal court this past weekend. Interesting."

"I have to be happy for him," Frank said. "But it means I'll have to find another senior warden. Why is it that just when everything is going along like a well-oiled machine something happens to throw it all off-kilter?''

"Are you speaking of the parish or your love life?" the bishop asked.

Frank squirmed uneasily in his chair. "Probably both."

"Well, you can't do anything about the first," His Eminence said. "And I think it's about time you did something about the other."

"But she's a lawyer and she lives here in Atlanta." Frank could hear panic in his own voice.

"Frank, you're just out of practice!" the bishop said with a laugh.

Frank glared at him for a moment, but then he had to laugh. "Yes, out of practice. And terrified. She's very attractive and smart, and one of the few women I've ever met who don't seem intimidated by the collar."

"She sounds too good for you," the bishop teased. "Frank, a man needs a helpmate for this job. When one is put in front of you, with such qualities as Rebecca Hobbs has, it's not wise to let her get away—providing that the feeling is there. It is there, isn't it?"

"Unfortunately, yes."

"Since when have you backed away from a challenge, son?"

Frank took a deep breath. "Can we get back to the parish problems?"

Rebecca threw the ad section of the newspaper into the garbage can outside the fast-food place where she'd gotten a late lunch. Nothing had even vaguely panned out. The offices she'd called on were ugly and characterless. The positions were glorified clerking jobs with little meaningful involvement.

She went back to her apartment and spotted a familiar white pickup truck in the parking lot near her own marked space. With a disbelieving heart, she scrambled out of her car and looked up at the balcony near the door to her apartment.

Frank Andrews stood there in full black regalia, a devastating silhouette leaning against the railing and reading a newspaper.

She ran up the steps and skidded to a stop in front of him. "Where've you been, so dressed up on a Monday?" Rebecca asked, getting out her key and unlocking the door.

"I had to take a report to the bishop here in Atlanta," he said, folding up the paper and following her into the cool dimness.

"I have to confess I've lapsed these past few years," Rebecca said, dumping her briefcase on the desk and kicking off her shoes. "In law school, Sunday was a good day to study. Now that I have a house to run I find it's the best time to get groceries. Anyway, I'm not up on church happenings. Who is the bishop now?"

Frank said nothing. When she looked over at him, he flexed his jaw. "Hey, have you forgotten his name so soon?" she asked. "You just saw him a few hours ago."

"It's Andrews," Frank said. "Nelson Andrews."

"Oh! Where have I heard that name before?" Rebecca asked.

"He's my father."

"No wonder you didn't mail your report, then—which was my next question."

Her glibness covered up the thoughts that were tumbling through her mind. "Why did he stick you out in a place like Blakesley Hills?" Rebecca asked. "Better yet, why did he let you go to the tropics and ruin your health?"

"Second question first," Frank said with a sigh. "He wasn't bishop when I went into the field. I got into that all by myself, and, looking back on it, I'm glad I did. When I came back, Father had that assignment and a slot on his staff. I chose Blakesley Hills."

"Ever the independent heart!" Rebecca said with a laugh.

"I resisted the call to the ministry as long as I could," Frank told her. "I was the typical preacher's kid, the exact opposite of what I was raised to be, until logic told me I was doing everything all wrong and that I was just making myself miserable by denying the path that had been set for me."

Rebecca nodded. "So you gave in, went to seminary, did the most noble thing you could do and became a missionary."

"Probably."

"Given another choice, you again chose to be noble."

"As best as I could."

"Hmmm! You show real character, Frank Andrews," she said, patting his shoulder. "Have you had your lunch?"

"Yes, thank you," Frank said, looking around her neat little living room. "With my mother."

"Oh? Good. I think I can find us some iced tea—"

"I called twice to see if you could meet us," he said, his voice resounding with a desolateness he had to be feeling. "Then, when I called again and you didn't answer, I thought you would probably come back pretty soon."

"With all due respect to your mother, who's probably a lovely person, I don't think I'm quite ready to meet your parents yet!" Rebecca said.

"You don't seem the least bit surprised to see me," Frank said as he followed her to the tiny kitchen.

"Only slightly," Rebecca said, covering what she really felt with a light tone.

"I called your folks last night, hoping to catch you before you left to arrange a lunch," he explained. "And your mother—"

"Gave you my address and detailed directions—"

"Not quite. I had to worm the information out of her."

She looked up at him from the pitcher of instant tea she was making and saw the devilish look in his eyes. "And if I believe that one . . ."

"She said something about your having to look for a new job."

"Well, if you must know, as of now I'm unemployed," Rebecca told him, opening the freezer to take out some ice. "I've spent this morning visiting offices that are less attractive than the one I'm leaving, and the work is even less challenging."

Frank leaned his shoulder against the doorway and studied her thoughtfully. "So this is what you'd left unsaid the whole time you were home?"

"Well, yes, I guess so," she said, filling two tall glasses. "I didn't think it mattered, between us."

Frank ran his hand through his thick black hair. "I thought maybe you had a man back here that you didn't want me to know about. That's the way a demented mind works, you know."

Rebecca laughed and handed a glass to him, then led him to the dining area, which looked out on the courtyard in the center of the apartment complex.

Frank put his glass down on the table and started to take off his suit jacket. A thick manila envelope fell from the inside pocket, and he looked at it for a moment before tucking it back into its place.

He sat down across the small table from her and looked around at her apartment from that aspect. "This is a nice place," he said.

Rebecca frowned. "Maybe it's because I've just come back from home, but it seems sort of…artificial to me. Too new. No character."

"How can it have no character if you're here?" Frank asked, smiling back at her.

"Cute. Going home has never affected me like this before. Since I've been back, I've been complaining about the traffic and the jobs and…even this place. And I used to love this apartment. Do you hear confession?" she asked.

Frank paused before drinking his tea. "Sure."

"I did something—something very out of character for me today. I blackmailed my soon-to-be-former boss for more severance pay than he was going to give me. I've turned into a hateful person here."

Frank reached out to take her hand. "Different games have different rules."

"I felt justified!" Rebecca said. "I don't like it here anymore. Jonathan—he's the vice president—said I've lost part of my edge and I should go back home to regain it. I did, and now I'm not at home here anymore."

"This sounds like something you'll have to work out for yourself," Frank said with a serious shake of his head.

"Now, why did you come here?"

"Do I need a reason?" he asked. "I needed to see your face. The past twenty-four hours have been the longest day I have ever been through."

Rebecca clasped her hands in front of her and rested her chin on her thumbs, gazing at him attentively. "It hasn't been easy on me, either," she said.

"I've been trying to see things from your perspective," Frank said. "We barely know each other, and I start talking about things like marriage. As far as you can see, there's really nothing to recommend me except that my cause is just and my heart is pure. You were perfectly right to call time-out, if not call the game off entirely. On the other hand, this is your home, and you have to follow your own calling. You're right to look ahead at what life is like for most ministers' wives and draw your own conclusions before you have too much invested in a relationship.''

''You make me sound heartless and calculating,'' Rebecca said. ''I'm also trying to spare you the embarrassment of being married to someone who was a bit of a character. Is it going to be any problem to you that I've had such high visibility back home? I'm just not the mousy type.''

''I think anything you've done in the past is surely overshadowed by the person you've become. The whole town of Blakesley Hills is talking about your coup with Mrs. Gruber's house—''

''Is this just selective listening, or do you have an objective source?''

''Granted, your Aunt Ruth might be biased, but I respect Thelma Pettigrew's opinions.''

Rebecca chuckled and stood up to replenish their tea. ''Yes, I suspect she does have her finger on the pulse of Blakesley Hills.''

Frank followed her to the kitchen. ''Becca, I'm committed to living up to the highest standards in my personal relationships. I don't have any qualms about loving you. Why should you have such doubts about yourself?''

''I guess they're about gone,'' she said.

''Look, I could arrange to come see you once a week or so. There's no pattern to the time I have free, but maybe Sunday afternoons.''

It might have been acceptable to a lesser woman, but Rebecca wasn't about to relegate the most important relationship she'd ever had to one afternoon a week. She made up her mind.

"That's sweet, Frank," she said. "But it might not be enough, unless you throw in Sunday evening, too."

"You drive a hard bargain, Rebecca." Frank laughed and hauled her into his arms. He kissed her until she gasped for breath, then turned his head to kiss her throat.

Rebecca closed her eyes and allowed her fingers to wander into the silken strands of his hair. Before she could get any sense of equilibrium he broke away and stood looking down at her now with a teasing fire in his dark eyes.

"I know you probably have other things to do today, and I'm in the way. I need to get back to Blakesley Hills."

So do I, Rebecca thought.

She reached into her pocket and found the piece of paper on which Jonathan had written the name of a professional headhunter. She stared at the name for a long moment, then made her decision. Plunging her hand back in her pocket, she watched Frank leave. He wasn't even all the way to his truck before she'd dug out the old Blakesley Hills telephone directory she kept on the shelf in her closet. After one phone call, the piece of paper was in the wastebasket.

Chapter Eleven

Bright and early the next morning, Rebecca arrived at the office of Minnifield, Drake and Hobbs. It was the same old place, cool and hushed, rows of law books wherever there was a place for them. Beyond the clatter of typewriters and word processors, there was the whir of ceiling fans and the buzz of telephones, all muffled by a tradition she could almost touch.

"Becky!" Miss Ives exclaimed, looking up from her desk. "Well, look at you. A big-city lawyer coming back to her old hometown."

"I'm here to see Mr. Minnifield and Mr. Drake. Are they in?"

"It just so happens they both *are* in at the moment," Miss Gilson said, picking up the telephone. "Now, let's see...Mr. Drake says for you to come back to his office, and when Mr. Minnifield is free I'll send him over."

Rebecca smiled and went down the hall to Edwin Drake's office. He sat behind his cluttered desk, his suit jacket slung over the back of his chair and his shirtsleeves rolled up.

"Well, young lady, I was afraid you weren't going to take our offer seriously," he said, waving a hand toward a chair. "As you can see, I've got a pile of work you could just dive right into."

"I hardly think you want me to do that," Rebecca said with a laugh.

"What kind of contract are you under now?" Drake asked, getting right to business.

"I'm free as soon as I clean out my desk," she told him.

He leaned back in his chair, then looked up at the door. Walt Minnifield stood there, his hand on the doorknob.

"I suppose you'll want a vacation after that." Walt said.

"No, this is my vacation. I have a few personal things to finish up in Atlanta, and then—" She spread her hands in explanation.

"We could put you to work Thursday morning," Ed said in the deep, full voice that resounded so well in a court-room.

"What about a buy-in?" Rebecca asked. "I'm getting a severance from my last employer."

The men looked at each other and Ed scratched his chin. "When we started the firm, Rebecca, it was a handshake deal. Put your severance in the bank."

Rebecca nodded. "What type of work do you want me to do?"

"All right." Walt said, "This is what we have in mind."

Rebecca settled back in her chair and listened.

"Just a tad up on your end, Frank," Tim sang out, his eyes intent on the level, which rested on a clapboard shin-gle.

Frank took a breath of the hot August air and hoisted the shingle a fraction of an inch. "How's that?" he called back.

"You got it!" Tim said approvingly, removing the level before Frank and Jim started pounding nails into the shingle.

They had done more work that morning than he'd expected. Tim and Jim were in the best mood he'd ever seen them in. Their two-day fishing trip had left them with two weeks' worth of funny stories to tell.

"Two more shingles and we'll be finished here," Frank said. "We'll break for lunch and do the trim and the roof this afternoon."

He was busy pounding away when he heard a car pull into the drive. Assuming it was Margaret Hobbs returning from the women's meeting at the church, he went on working.

"Hello up there!" It was Rebecca's voice.

Frank looked down and clutched the side of his ladder for support. "What the—dickens are you doing here?"

"I live here, you know," she responded in a teasing tone. "Morning, boys. How was the fishing?"

"Fine!"

"Great!"

"Boys, when you're at a good stopping place, I need some things carried into the house."

"Yes, ma'am," they chorused eagerly.

"This can wait until after lunch, guys," Frank said, eager to get down the ladder and within hugging distance of Rebecca.

"Nope," Tim said. His grin told Frank that he was about to get a taste of his own discipline. "Let's get it done now."

"No sense stopping so close to having it done," Jim agreed.

Frank grumbled inwardly about training the boys a bit too well as he went back to work. It took supreme concentra-

tion to stay on the ladder when he could feel Rebecca
watching him.

"I suppose Mama's still at church?" she asked.

"I suppose so," Frank replied, muscling the last shingle
into place.

"A little higher on your end, Frank," Tim instructed.
"That's got it."

Frank pounded the last nail with a little more energy than
necessary and clambered down the ladder as quickly as he
could. The boys took her bags from the trunk of her car and
carried them into the house with their usual lack of cere-
mony.

Rebecca looked very official in a gray skirt and a white
blazer, the collar of a red blouse just peeking out. She also
had a smile that meant that a canary was in deep trouble.

"All right, you've tortured me long enough," he said.
"What are you up to?"

"I got a new job," she said.

"So soon? I thought you were pretty discouraged yesterday."

"I'd had a previous offer I decided to take," she told him.
"Ed Drake and Walt Minnifield offered me a junior partnership in their firm."

"What? Here in Blakesley Hills?"

Rebecca shrugged nonchalantly, then burst out laughing
and threw her arms around him. "I'm going to be writing
wills for little old ladies and trying to keep troublemaking
rapscallions out of court and seeing that justice is done."

He was conscious of the grime on his hands, and he resisted the temptation to return her embrace, though it took
a great effort. He kissed her. "Congratulations!" he managed.

"Come in and have lunch with me," Rebecca said. "I
think I've got this all figured out. I'll live here and sublet my

place to my folks until they find a place they like in Atlanta.''

''Where do you want these bags?'' one of the twins called from inside the house.

''Top of the back stairs, boys,'' she answered, entering the kitchen and taking off her jacket. Her sleeveless red blouse showed off the golden tan she'd gotten the week before.

The boys' sneakered feet sounded like thunder as they ran back down the back stairs. ''Want us to get the rest of the stuff?'' Tim asked.

''Yes, please,'' Rebecca called after them, opening the refrigerator and taking out a pitcher of lemonade. ''Go ahead and wash up at the sink there, Frank. I'll get you a fresh towel....''

He chuckled to himself. She was just like her mother, unflappable and able to do everything at once. He was toweling off when the boys finished their second trip and Rebecca told them the rest of her things could wait until later.

''Run on home, boys,'' Frank said, leaning against the counter. Jim just waved and left, but Tim grinned knowingly and let the screen door slam behind him.

''You're a dangerous man, Frank Andrews,'' Rebecca said, coming up behind him as he hung the towel on the rack over the sink.

''How so?'' he asked, looking back over his shoulder.

''You've caused a thoroughly sensible woman's life to career wildly out of control,'' she told him seriously. He frowned at her, and she laughed.

''Rebecca, I didn't intend—'' he began, turning to catch her bare arms in his broad hands. ''You've made a tremendous sacrifice for a relationship that might not work out.''

''Sacrifice!'' She laughed and slipped her arms around his waist. ''The biggest sacrifice I'm making is that I'll have to

find someone who can cut my hair like this. Maybe I'll let
it grow long...."

"I love it just the way it is," he said, kissing a strand of
her hair as it brushed her forehead.

"I love you just the way *you* are," Rebecca said. "Generous to a fault, quick-tempered, God-fearing and totally
honest. I just had to come back here and protect you from
yourself and every marriageable female in the county."

Frank tried to think of something profound to say, but he
decided actions would speak better than any words. He
kissed Rebecca with more ardor than he thought he was capable of. And she responded in kind, breaking away only
when she heard her mother's car pull into the yard.

"Later," she said, her eyes flashing, as she wiped lipstick from his mouth with gentle fingers.

He kissed her forehead and let her go. "Let me get this
straight," he said. "You're coming home to work in your
dad's old firm."

"Yes?" Rebecca said, puzzled.

"Need a client?"

"I'll do anything the church needs *pro bono*."

"It's not for the church," he said. "It's for me."

Rebecca shrugged. "Sure. Anything."

"The papers are in the glove compartment of my truck,"
Frank told her. "I'll be right back."

He passed Margaret on his way out the door, and from
the look on her face he could see that she was as surprised
to see that Rebecca had returned as he'd been. When he got
back to the kitchen, they were hugging each other and
making plans about something or other.

"You will stay for lunch, won't you, Frank?" Margaret
said. "You both go sit down while I take care of everything."

Rebecca eyed the bulky manila envelope he handed her and looked back at him. "Let's go into Daddy's study," she suggested. "This looks important."

She led him across the hall to the study and closed the door behind them. "Have a seat and I'll see what I can do for you."

Sitting down at her father's desk, she removed the contents of the envelope and surveyed the legal document with a curiosity that quickly turned to surprise.

"This is a trust fund," she said.

"Yes. While my father's side of the family tends to theology, my mother's likes to make money," Frank told her. "My grandfather set up a trust fund for me, and since I was a bit of a character when I was younger he stipulated that I not have control of it until I turned thirty, hoping I'd have some sense by then. Next month, to be exact."

"Well, ah, this is based on some securities," Rebecca said, going on to the next page. "Quite a variety of industrial stocks, with dividends that have accumulated over the last…fifteen years." Her breath caught. "Um-hum! What do you want me to do with this?"

"I'll want to know how much it's worth," Frank said. "I need to replace the truck. Then I'll start looking for a house to buy. There's a place on Butler Street that I really like."

Rebecca studied a few more paragraphs of the document and folded it again. "I think that, with prudence, you can take care of that."

"My grandfather thought I'd squander all the money if he didn't encumber it. So many times when I was in the field I wished that I could have given more than my time and work to the people I was trying to help. But money wasn't enough to solve their long-term problems, I learned. When His Eminence assigned me here, he knew I'd soon have an independent income. It's just been tough getting to the light at the end of the tunnel.''

"Let me see what I can do about setting up a monthly income for you, with some idea of what you have to put down on a vehicle," Rebecca said, scribbling a note on the fresh pad in front of her. "Then I'll see what you might look forward to as a down payment on a house.''

"Good," Frank said, getting to his feet and coming around the desk to perch on the arm of her chair.

"You're going to keep on doing carpentry?" Rebecca asked, looking up at him.

"Why not?" Frank said, resting his hand on her shoulder. "I have to keep busy, and it helps me meet the people around here and get to know them."

"I hope you know how much I love you," she said.

"Oh, yes, I know how much you love me," he said. "I learned long ago not to tell anyone about that little document until and unless I knew their motives very well. You passed with flying colors, Miss Rebecca." He kissed her thoroughly. "I hope you're not angry with me for wanting to be sure of you before I shared this with you."

The smile on her face changed. "I knew in my heart I couldn't exist seeing you once a week. I don't believe in a lot of the things you do, but I do believe we met for a purpose, and if it leads to marriage I won't be scared off. That's a warning.''

"I'll remember that when I'm ready to ask you," Frank said, bending down to kiss her soft mouth.

"Until then, I'll practice saying *yes*!"

Epilogue

The church had never been packed with such a distinguished congregation of clergy, officers of the courts and prominent citizens. Rebecca had thought she would be nervous, but she couldn't feel anything but at ease while her mother methodically presided over the staging of the wedding.

In her mauve lace frock, Margaret puffed the organza sleeves of Rebecca's white gown, then made certain that the wide satin skirt and train lay just right. "I never thought Aunt Ruth could make the embroidery and beading turn out this well."

Indeed, Aunt Ruth had outdone herself, creating a gown that reflected Rebecca's innate élan and elegance.

Rebecca saw the loving look that passed between her parents just before Margaret lowered her veil and handed her the bridal bouquet of white roses and calla lilies. She placed her hand on Big Ted's arm and watched Margaret disappear beyond the vestibule doors with her brother.

When the doors opened again and she saw Frank and his attendants enter, she was in control of herself. She caught her breath when she saw how handsome he looked in formal clothes.

"Does he always wear black, white and gray?" she asked his younger sister, Lynn, who was a bridesmaid.

Lynn adjusted the bodice of her yellow taffeta gown. "Except for the briefs I sent him when he was in the field," she whispered.

Rebecca's eyes were glittering when she reached him at the front of the church, and she could barely control a giggle.

A deep breath made the lapels of Frank's jacket rise. Then he shook his head and expelled a breath like an athlete about to attempt some great feat, dazzled by this woman who never ceased to amaze him.

They both turned toward Bishop Andrews, who smiled down at them, his hand poised on his prayer book.

"Rebecca? Are you sure you want to marry this fellow?" Bishop Andrews asked in a stage whisper. "Believe me, he's no bargain."

"I'll take my chances," Rebecca said, shooting a sidelong glance at Frank.

Bishop Andrews turned toward Frank. "Frank, last chance to chicken out."

Frank grinned down at Rebecca. "No, this is what I want."

"All right. We have to get serious here," the bishop said, straightening his shoulders and assuming a very solemn demeanor.

Frank took Rebecca's hand and mouthed the words *I love you*.

Rebecca pursed her lips into a kiss in the air.

The bishop's voice filled the nave of the little church. "Dearly beloved . . ."

*   *   *   *   *

A compelling novel of deadly revenge and passion
from bestselling international
romance author Penny Jordan

POWER PLAY

Eleven years had passed but the
terror of that night was something
Pepper Minesse would never
forget. Fueled by revenge against
the four men who had brutally
shattered her past, she set in
motion a deadly plan to destroy
their futures.

Available in February!

**At long last, the books you've been waiting for
by one of America's top romance authors!**

DIANA PALMER
DUETS

Ten years ago Diana Palmer published her very first
romances. Powerful and dramatic, these gripping tales
of love are everything you have come to expect from
Diana Palmer.

In March, some of these titles will be available again in
DIANA PALMER DUETS—a special three-book collection. Each book will have two wonderful stories plus an
introduction by the author. You won't want to miss them!

Book 1
**SWEET ENEMY
LOVE ON TRIAL**

Book 2
**STORM OVER THE LAKE
TO LOVE AND CHERISH**

Book 3
**IF WINTER COMES
NOW AND FOREVER**

 *Silhouette Books*®

Diana Palmer brings you an Award of Excellence title... and the first Silhouette Romance DIAMOND JUBILEE book.

ETHAN
by Diana Palmer

In January 1990, Diana Palmer continues her bestselling LONG, TALL TEXANS series with *Ethan*—the story of a rugged rancher who refuses to get roped and tied by Arabella Craig, the one woman he can't resist.

The Award of Excellence is given to one specially selected title per month. Spend January with *Ethan* #694... a special DIAMOND JUBILEE title... only in Silhouette Romance.